Beautiful

Shadows

Jonathan G. Alterio

Jonathan G. Alterio

Beautiful Shadows

It was a dark summer evening and Charles was just leaving the library. He just finished his research into the Draco crime family. Charles was average height with dark blonde hair. Not overly athletic and slender with even proportions. In his arms he had a mix of documents he complied from public sources mixed in with other documents acquired from less reputable sources which contained inside information about the Mob boss and his operations. Charles stood atop the steps to the library entrance waiting for his sister, Carinne. A cool breeze was blowing the papers in his arms causing him to tighten his grip. Off in the distance he sees her silhouette and raises an arm waving over to her which she spots and returns the wave. The street had many dark spots due to the combination of the moonless night and several non-functioning street lamps. From that darkness a figure emerged, his facial features were hidden due to the lack of light. He wore a fedora and long coat which he began to peel open. Everything seemed to be occurring in slow motion and as the coat was folding away it occurred to Charles in that brief moment that this was possibly one of Draco's men, he immediately turned towards Carinne who was making her way towards him hastily and he yelled "RUN!" waving one hand in a gesture pointing her in the opposite direction. She stopped dead in her tracks and heard a gunshot. Charles was turning to run back into the library for shelter but the gunman fired hitting him in the back and Charles stumbled and fell. Carinne let out a scream so loud that it echoed for a few blocks, anyone within ear shot stopped what they were doing wherever they were and started looking around trying to isolate its source. A few people that were outside ran over to her and others from within the library began running out. The gunman tried to wrestle the papers from Charles but now there were witnesses. Seeing that he had little time to escape he ceased the struggle, left Charles bleeding and dying, and ran off as fast as he could. Carinne ran over and grabbed her brother's hand.

"Don't die please! You have to hang on!" She yelled through

tears.

"Carinne, take these, give them to the authorities, promise me you will…"

His hand went limp. One of the bystanders ran up followed by another then another.

She grabbed the papers and stood up. In the darkness, not too far off, a car slowly drives close to the scene to try to get a read of the people present but more importantly who has the papers, then drives off before attracting any attention.

Later that night at the hospital, Carinne was replaying the events that just occurred over and over again in her head. She had ridden in the ambulance with her dying brother. They had managed to resuscitate him once but were unable to do so again. She held the papers he handed to her tightly, many of them splattered with blood. She finished her business at the hospital upon the pronouncement of his death and met with the officers who arrived to give statements about what she witnessed. With the harshest aspects of the night seemingly behind her she paced back and forth in the lobby waiting for the cab to arrive. The ride home was the longest ride she ever had. The cab driver may have been talking to her, but all she heard was a muffled voice, everything was a blur. She rode back with her head slumped to one side nearly against the door window starring out focusing on nothing. As the cab pulled into her driveway, up in the tree above her yard, a large figure loomed looking down. He watched Carinne exit the cab, then after it drove off the figure dropped down and ran towards the door trying to catch Carinne, but the door closed on him.

Inside Carinne dropped the paperwork on the nearest table then heard a knock. She spun around shocked and looked through the peep hole.

"Hello Carinne, I know It's late and I know what you just went through but you're in danger, we need to talk."

"Who are you?"

"I am here to help and protect you. There are others on their way here. The ones that murdered your brother."

Before she could respond she heard someone upstairs.

"There's someone in my house." She said out loud.

"That's my team Carinne, they will help you escape. We are running out of time."

Behind her two people emerged, both women, both dressed in black fatigues, the first held out her hand towards Carinne."

"It's ok honey, come with us so we can protect you. You can't stay here."

She was trapped at this point so she opened the front door.

"Hello Carinne. My name is Willhaven. We are known as shadows and we work to help people in danger. I need you to please leave with them, there is…"

Willhaven was interrupted, another person came running towards him. It was another one of his shadow team members, he had a pair of binoculars he tucked back into his coat as he approached, and he was also dressed fully in black and masked.

"Will, there's a car driving towards us, it's not far, we need to all go RIGHT NOW!"

Willhaven nodded. He put on his mask as well. He signaled to the two inside and they pulled Carinne with them and left out the back door grabbing the blood stained papers on their way out. Willhaven turned around and ran back from where he dropped and with incredible athleticism climbed back up into the tree. His accomplice shadow also returned to his spot high up on Carinne's roof top and hunched behind the rise so only his head protruded. A minute or so afterwards the car had pulled up. Willhaven performed hand signals to the shadow on the roof top. The hand signals were asking if the subject, Carinne, was safe. The shadow turned to communicate with another that was further back but out of Willhaven's view. The signals that were returned to Willhaven indicated that Carinne was not yet in the clear. He needed to do something. Looking down he saw the driver emerge then two large men from the back seat. He prepared his steel darts. He had heavy darts that were more like weighted steel spikes. He launched the first at the driver's head, then another at one gunman's head and the third at the last gunman's head. The first two fell dead as the dart's tip penetrated their skulls but the third gunman had luck on his side. He had moved at the moment Willhaven released the dart causing it to impale him in his shoulder. All of this happened very quickly but Willhaven was ready. As the last gunman looked up he caught an eye full of Willhaven's immense cloaked figure descending on him. Willhaven's nearest shadow accomplice saw a second car pulling up. He looked over at Willhaven then looked over to the other shadow team member. The hand signals returned from this other shadow indicated that Carinne was now secure. The first shadow responded back indicating that Willhaven was surrounded and in danger. Down on the ground below Willhaven was wrestling with the gunman, he had removed the dart and was stabbing him in the heart. He used all his strength to push past the gunman's resistance, all arms were locked but Willhaven over came him and killed him. Four large armed men now jump out of the second car and rush Willhaven, even if the other shadows were to get involved at this point they would all die possibly as they would be outnumbered. Could he do anything he thought? Their code forbade reckless jeopardy of their lives when the outcome is known. He motioned to move but now Willhaven was being overcome. Willhaven fought one, knocking him off balance then another disarming him and the third he grappled with but now he was overcome. He was tied and tossed into the trunk. Maybe he could toss a dart to get their attention? The shadow thought. He paused. Confusion filled him momentarily.

He recovered his composure and the hand signals began again, he sent the instruction to follow that car NOW! The two figures dropped from the darkness they were hiding in, the one closest to Willhaven kept out of view of the car as it was driving off but began to build a picture in his mind of the car's details and license plate. The other went into Carinne's home looking for car keys. As he shuffled around the home his ally ran in towards the phone and made a call. Once someone answered on the hot line, the car's description was given to them and they were made aware that Willhaven was captured.

"Found it!" One of the shadow's said jingling the car keys.

"I phoned it in, others on the team will be looking for that car as well."

"Let's see if we can catch up to them!"

They both jump in the car and the tires scream their way on to the street in hot pursuit. The car carrying Willhaven pulled up to a warehouse in a dark area of the city. Willhaven had left severe dents in the trunk during his attempts trying to kick it open.

"Be careful with this one, he's gotta a lotta strength." One of the thugs warned.

The kicking was still occurring when Willhaven's last kick flung the trunk open hitting one of them square in the face as he unlocked the trunk.

"Good timing asshole!" he yelled at him.

It took all four to wrestle him out of the trunk and restrain him on to a special table fitted with straps for the arms and legs.

One of the thugs grabbed a nearby phone and called their boss.

"Hey Draco, we got someone here that attacked us. We were trying to pickup the girl when we were jumped. He killed three of our men!"

"What about the girl?" Draco asked stoically.

"We don't got her."

"I'll get another car to go to the house. I want you to get all information from this guy, use all methods and get it quick then get rid of him."

The line clicked and the thug hung up.

"Well Well, it looks like it's your lucky day." He said looking at Willhaven.

Willhaven was still trying to break the new bonds that tied him to the table but it was not possible.

From behind he heard the sound of wind blowing out of a hose. No wait, he smelled gas. No, now he heard a click and wind became heat. He tilted his head to one side and a torch came into view as one of the thugs stepped from behind Willhaven.

"Listen, your gonna tell us everything you know and this fire here is gonna help you talk." The thug removed the wraps preventing Willhaven from speaking or screaming. Then he moved in and began burning one of Willhaven's hands, just enough to show he was serious. Willhaven was sweating and his jaw was tight and teeth clenched.

"Oh I see, you think you handle the pain? Ok then how about this."

The thug turns the flame on high and now begins cooking Willhaven's hand. He watched as Willhaven twisted in place still trying to rip free of the binds, but no scream came, only grunts. He brought the flame in closer as the hand continued to cook. It was now completely scorched and black. Pieces of skin falling off. No screams, no talking, Willhaven remained silent. The thug moves to the next hand and went to work but Willhaven uttered no words.

"Maybe fire's not gonna work. Let's try the sledge."

The thug grabs a sledgehammer then pounds Willhaven's left foot to a pulp. The grunts come much louder but no screaming and no talking. He moves on to the next foot. He took his time, first hammering the toes, then the top of the foot then the ankle. When he did not get the response he wanted he hammered both shins breaking the bone and pushing it through the flesh.

Willhaven lost consciousness at this point and was bleeding badly.

"He's not gonna talk and he's not gonna make it." The thug said putting the hammer down.

"We need to get rid of this body quick." Said another.

They tied Willhaven back up and tossed him in the trunk of another car. Down at the other end of the street the two shadows drove slowly into view as they saw Willhaven's abductors.

"Slow down! They are leaving with Will again!!" The shadow in the passenger seat said.

"I see them, let's wait and follow."

When the thugs resumed driving the shadows would follow far enough behind to not lose them but also not close enough to be noticed. They drove until they reached a high ridge overlooking a river. They saw the thugs pull over and jump out immediately.

"It looks like they gonna weigh him down and toss him in!"

"We gotta do something!"

The two shadows covered their faces and resumed driving down to the road.

"Maybe we can ram the car?" The passenger said.

The thugs were focused on preparing Willhaven's burial but then one of them noticed headlights in the distance.

"Hey, do you see that!" One of the thugs yelled.

"Yea it's a car. It's coming this way!"

"Fuck it, leave him. He'll be dead anyway. Let's get outta here quick before they get nosy."

"He look, they are getting back in the car!." The shadow in the driver's seat said. As the thugs left, the two shadows pulled up. They parked the car and ran over to Willhaven, mutilated and unconscious but still alive.

"Quick get him in!"

They grabbed him, one by the shoulders and the other hugged the waist. The ends of the arms and legs were destroyed, bleeding. They placed him in the back seat carefully and gently.

"We need to bring him our medic lab." The driver said.

"It's further away than the hospital though."

"We have no choice." The driver said then they sped off.

***

The orderlies rushed Willhaven into a special operating room. It was located in the VARS headquarters in Hope City. VARS stands for Victim Assistance and Relocation Society. The shadows worked for them, aiding with risky rescues and providing protection from dangerous criminals. Willhaven is a shadow warrior, their leader in fact. The shadow program operated covertly to support saving victims that have been identified as definite targets for assassination or other similar harms. Willhaven's charge was to save Carinne but now finds himself needing rescuing.

"Blood pressure is very low." Called out the nurse reading the vitals.

"His records indicate he is allergic to anesthetics." Called another reading his papers.

"Do we know which?" This came from a doctor who joined the team.

In the operating room, Willhaven is placed on the operating table.

"Use conscious sedation." Said the doctor.

Willhaven regained consciousness to find an oxygen mask over his mouth. He raised one of his arms in a gesture meant to remove the mask but was horrified when he saw that no fingers remained, only cooked nubs. Anger swelled. He began to remember. The sedatives had reduced the physical pain, but Willhaven would let out a series of screams that would deafen anyone near him. To the staff that was present it sounded like muttering mixed in with screams but then they made out some words. At the top of his lungs he would scream "I WILL KILL YOU DRACO!" and in short time his voice would become raspy from the exertion. He looked down and saw what was done to his legs. Then more screams. "ALL OF THEM WILL DIE!".

"More sedatives, and strap him down. We can't have him flailing for what comes next."

They wrestled his arms back as he screamed, enraged. Peering through glass windows looking in on the scene was Stephen Kline, the lead neurologist. He became very unsettled by the screams and decided to put on some Mozart and turned the volume up to drown it out. Willhaven stopped screaming when he heard the music faintly. He threw a horrific glance over at Stephen who was on the opposite side of the glass window. He yelled and screamed more until his vocal cords no longer supported it and would never support it again. This did not stop Willhaven from mouthing silent screams and threats. The silence caused Stephen to look back over to Willhaven. One of the doctors nearby spoke to Willhaven.

"Will, we must perform amputations to save you. We have sedated you as much as we can. When we are done you will have some bionics to aid you with day-to-day life."

Willhaven looked over with a mad glance breathing heavily. He shot breaths at the doctor as he no longer had a voice but then turned his head back and reclined staring at the ceiling. The operations began and would continue for the next few months slowly reconstructing his limbs.

***

Willhaven was walking towards the office of the head of the VARS program, Terrance Leighwind III. Terrance was 70 years old and very sickly. He was short and a bit fat with straight white hair and a white short beard. He was a dying man with a dying wish to better the world and had the money to deliver on it. He is the founder of VARS and the last in his family line. His only Child died of a rare illness and his wife passed away several years ago.

"Hello Will. It's good to see you have fully recovered."

"I suppose." His voice was artificially rendered from a voice box and was crackling as he spoke.

"Yes, that's actually why I asked to have you come see me. We have prosthetics that can make your life…. somewhat normal again."

"Somewhat is not good enough and I also have unfinished business." He crackled in response.

"You have a tough soul Will, but you no longer have the capability to support us in your old role in the same manner."

Willhaven raised his arms and looked at his elbows. There was no arm past that point only a circular ring with some connectors that looked like something could be bolted on.

"Yes, your arms. We have some great robotics that…"

Willhaven cut him off and asked "I heard about battle robotics from Mr. Kline."

"Oh, is that so? We have that but it's experimental. Did he also mention that."

"Yes, he did but that is a risk I am willing to take. I can help push it to the next level."

Terrance rubbed his beard and considered the situation.

"Will, you would become a guinea pig as this technology has not been tested on any humans. I don't have the same level of confidence as Mr. Kline, and I commend your resolve. I can't conceive of allowing testing and experimenting on any human."

"I have probably the highest pain threshold of anyone. If things start to go wrong we can always back out."

Terrence tried to hide his pleasure, but a faint smile made its way to Willhaven. The next evolution in the VARS program will use enhancements for their shadows however the plan was to make battle suits. What was being considered here was skipping an evolutionary step in the development process. Terrence did not expect to live long and knew he would not see this but now with Willhaven's cooperation and willingness to push the program forward he may just see it in his lifetime.

"I will discuss this matter with Stephen. I will also have him fix your voice box in the mean time."

"Thank you Mr. Leighwind but there's nothing wrong with my voice box. I was told it amplifies what is coming from what's left of my voice and the crackling is part of that. The device is only magnifying the sounds so I can be heard. I rather like it this way. It's a reminder of what I have been turned into."

Terrance nodded then turned and went back to his desk. Willhaven left as well. In a few days Willhaven, Stephen and Terrance would agree to begin a new operation to retrofit battle gear to Willhaven. New gear would be designed to interface with Willhaven's nervous system, what was not fully known to Willhaven yet was how this interface would operate.

***

A few months had passed and the gear was finally ready. Willhaven lay on a special stretcher that was attached to a larger machine. It was reminiscent of an MRI with a giant donut shaped mechanism at the head of the table. It was composed of small mechanical arms and miles of coiled exposed wiring, circuitry and special lighting. The mechanical arms had circuit board attachments at their base. At the end of the mechanical arm was a unique tool for each arm. One arm had forceps, another had surgical scissors, then there was a cluster of arms that each had unique types of artery forceps. Adjacent to these arms were a set of cleaning arms ready to disinfect the instruments before and after their use. This machine was known as the Brain Chip Integration Robot or (B.C.I.R). Its previous patients had been nothing more evolved than chimps, but now it is upgraded to work on humans.

Willhaven's arms and legs were strapped in and further restricted to prevent as little motion as possible. He was sedated similarly to before. Operating the machine were two neurologists and several doctors. Stephen Kline, the head neurologist, was monitoring the BCIR, and Willhaven from an adjacent room which contained the computer's expanded dashboards, controls and biological monitors. Sensors were connected to Willhaven's head to monitor brain activity and additional sensors were connected to his chest to keep on eye on his heart activity. As the program began execution the machine came to life with a low hum. The lights dimmed around the room; the only light was from the targeted beams from the BCIR. The table rotated mechanically quickly spinning Willhaven face down. The doctors stood back and the BCIR slowly slid into position over Willhaven's head stopping at his neck. The arms extended as part of the table folded up and away exposing Willhaven's upper back. Other mechanical arms, these with pads on the end, extended from under the table and supported Willhaven comfortably but firmly locking him into place. These pads alleviated pressure points and would move Willhaven into perfect positions.

The work began with needles going into Willhaven's neck just at the point where it crossed his collarbone known as the cervicothoracic junction. Two incisions were made on the left and right sides of the spine. Within these insertions a small flat chip was placed in each. The chip had exposed delicate wiring waiting to be connected. The mechanical arms then began inserting small rods into the spine delicately and quickly. They were inserted at different depths perfectly measured. Dr. Kline watched on his monitors as the work was being performed engrossed in awe at his own creation and its success so far. The monitor Dr. Kline was focused on currently allowed him to witness the rods being inserted into Willhaven's spinal area. The rod at this magnified view can be seen to be needle like but down the stem it had micro mechanical tendrils. These are not easily visible to the human eye but once the rod was in the spine these tendrils would attach to specific nerves when the command was sent. The rods were then connected to the chips and Dr. Kline then sent the command to activate this understructure. The tendrils came to life and found the nerve endings they would attach to. When they took grip, all at once, Willhaven let out a loud grunt then asked the operation to stop. Dr. Kline saw the reaction, immediately left the room and walked over.

"What's wrong?"

"That pain, it was extreme. I've never felt anything like that before."

Stephen looked at the heart monitor and it was very elevated but dropping.

"We can stop at any time Will, you just let us know and we can stop the whole procedure."

"Just give me sec."

"Sure."

Willhaven considered the pain. He thought to himself "let's try again."

"Dr. Kline, how much more of this is there?"

"Well, we will need to repeat this process a few times. We will then need to add the computer that will interface between your brain and body then connect that to your spine, that will hurt more."

"Proceed to the next step then." Willhaven said staring at the ground.

As the process moved along Willhaven would ask for a pause several more times. Eventually, however the artificially intelligent second brain was in Willhaven. It was installed in the cervicothoracic junction below the other components and the final connection needed to be made. At this point Stephen Kline walked over to discuss what would happen next.

"How are you feeling Will?"

Willhaven was sweating, the sedatives only did so much, and his heart rate was high but lowering again.

"We can keep it going. Just give me a few minutes."

"Will, this last step…It's the most painful. Everyone is here ready to support you. It will be very brief but very painful."

"I'm ready for it. Thanks for the warning." Willhaven mentally braced himself and tensed his muscles.

Dr. Kline walked back and stared at the heart rate monitor waiting for it to settle back down. He called over to Willhaven and said:

"Big pinch coming."

With the press of the button Mr. Kline instructed the BCIR to complete the operation. The new needles within Willhaven's neck and spine were all pressed in, and the tendrils all connected. The artificial intelligence chip in him came to life and took control and became the conduit in between his thoughts and actions.

Willhaven, though restrained, convulsed when this happened. His body arched, his heart monitor raced to the ceiling, then Willhaven relaxed and and flat lined.

The doctors present tried to resuscitate him, but it was hopeless. He was declared dead after a few minutes. All monitors now show flat lines. The artificial intelligence chip however was functioning and sending wavelengths. Stephen dismissed the doctors and thanked them for their participation. He ended the program which caused the BCIR to return Willhaven to his starting position face up on the table. Dr. Kline removed one monitor pad after another but before he could remove the last Willhaven began speaking.

"SSSSTTTTEEEEEEEPPPHHHENNNN" Came the crackling

voice.

Dr. Kline looked over and the heart monitor was still a flat line.

"Will is that you?" He asked.

"No Sttteeeepphhhen."

"Who are you then?"

The voice became steady now.

"Congratulations Stepphhhhenn. You have succeeded."

Stephen looked over again at the heart monitor but there was no change. "Could this be the artificial intelligence talking to me? No, it can't be it's not built to do this!" He thought to himself.

"Am I speaking to the chip?"

"Stephen, your mechanical wonder is not speaking to you now. We will meet when your time comes."

Stephen started walking backwards. He asked again:

"Who is this?"

"It is not your time yet, but it IS Willhaven's." The voice emphasized. It was raspy in addition to being crackly.

Stephen picked up the phone to call Terrance or any doctor, anyone that was nearby but when he grabbed the phone it burned his hand and he immediately dropped it. The voice called out again.

"Destroy all your work Stephen. Your toy goes no further, or your time will come sooner." It spoke.

The heart monitor began registering beats and returned to normal and Willhaven's chest slowly rose and fell with his breathing. He was still unconscious and would be for another day, but he was alive again.

***

Willhaven woke staring at the ceiling in one of the medical rooms. He heard a buzz then the door to his room opened with a click as Dr. Kline walked in. Willhaven raised his arms to stretch and saw them for the first time since the operation, the sight caused him to stop before reaching a full stretch to consider them more closely. He eyed them up and down. He was retrofitted with heavy duty battle prosthetics as he had desired. The extra weight pulled him into the bed as if he was sinking.

"Hello Will, we had a serious scare from you the other day."

"I don't remember anything except a moment of extreme pain then waking up here."

"You actually died Will. You were dead for several minutes."

"I assume it was you who resuscitated me then?"

"Actually, it appears that you resuscitated yourself. I have not seen anything like that before in my life but I'm glad you are doing well now."

"Were you aware of how much pain this operation was causing?"

"Remember Will, you are the first human. The highest life form to this point were chimps and they can be sedated fully."

"Mr. Kline. Your machine... This part of the VARS program…"

He trailed off unable to finish his thought.

"Excuse me Will. What are you trying to say?"

"This chip you placed in me. It's very strange. How does it work exactly?"

"It's an interface between your brain and your nervous system. It can react faster than your brain. You can also use it to control your prosthetics as if they were actual limbs. It can read your subconscious responses and convert it into actions. It can read your thoughts and answer logical questions. An example of a logical question suited to your new abilities might be something like how far of a fall can I take before it becomes fatal. With your new body you would suffer far less damage from far greater heights than any normal human. Have you seen your legs yet?"

"I think this computer goes beyond anything ethical Dr. Kline." His anger was rising but then it suddenly dropped before it could break through his stoic demeanor.

"Will, this is a miracle, we can't stop now. We shouldn't. This chip very likely is the reason you are alive!" He paused for just a second then continued.

"We have an incredible breakthrough. It just needs some more tweaks, and we will be able to enhance any human!"

"I don't share your sentiment. We can discuss it further at some other time. For now, I have some other questions."

He changed the subject to his new capabilities. His focus returning to his bionics.

"I have two slots under each arm, why?"

"That is for weaponry, the computer implanted in you can control any prosthetics it is connected to that we have designed. It can be various types of weaponry such as guns and lasers. These can attach to those slots."

At least there is a positive side to this, he thought to himself. He is now built to execute justice and fight crime better than he ever could.

"Can I see what armaments are available?"

"Absolutely, we can take a look after you get some more rest."

"Great."

"One last question Will. Have you ever spoken in your sleep?"

"No, never. Why did I do that?"

"No, never mind."

Willhaven eyed Stephen as he left the room, he felt a strange relaxation come over him. He resumed examination of his new arms.

At his elbows a new mechanical forearm and hands were connected. He moved them by thought alone as if they were his original human hands. He touched the table near his bed, running his mechanical fingers along the top but he could not feel anything. The vibrations sent a signal that the CPU received which was sent to his brain imitating sensation but it was not true feeling. It was better than nothing and it worked well enough so that he could identify many solid surfaces such as metal, plastic and glass. It could also communicate temperature. He knew the temperature of the room and even his own temperature.

He pulled the blanket completely off himself and saw that his lower legs were mechanical from the knee downward. Where his feet once were he now had mechanical boots. They were metal on rubber soles and had several levels of articulation his human feet did not have. At his knee there were hydraulic connections made to his torso. The chest portion had armor that contained circuitry underneath. The back portion ran down and narrowed and connected to the leg hydraulics. He needed the connection in order to walk but he could remove it if needed or desired. The computer in him let him know that there were some mechanisms to his feet. As he moved them around, he accidentally released a large blade from in between the toe section. He also learned he could rotate them 360 degrees. Excitement momentarily ran through him as he thought about how he would punish criminals, and especially how he would take down Draco and his crime syndicate.

He had a surreal feeling, unnatural even, that thoughts he was having might not be his own. The computer installed in him was acting invisibly but his awareness seemed other worldly. He could hear the most minute sounds in the room, one of which was an ant crawling on the floor, he looked in its direction, it was blurry at first but then he focused and he saw it clearly.

Can this computer read all his thoughts? Is it giving him ideas?? Yes…Another meeting with Kline is definitely due. His mind racing with all kinds of thoughts. Then he was suddenly relaxed again.

This computer must be controlling his brain juices. Willhaven was always in touch with his body and even though he is now part machine he still knew it was controlling him to some unknown degree which bothered him. Who knows what else it would do. This is not good. He took advantage of the relaxed state, closed his eyes and slept.

In Willhaven's sleep came a strange dream. He was standing alone in darkness. A spotlight was on him, it's source unidentifiable. Then he heard a voice:

"Willhaven, we have much work to do you and I."

"Yes, this city needs to be purged of its violence and malevolent forces but I work alone, it's too dangerous…" Willhaven responded.

"NO, we…work…. together!"

Willhaven was silent for a moment.

"Who are you?"

"I will be your guide."

"I..am…going…crazy."

"NO, you are not, but if we don't work together, you will. That toy that has been implanted in you is not compatible with human existence as you may already be sensing."

This statement caused Willhaven to reach back behind his neck and touch the pad where the CPU had been installed behind. His metal fingers only communicate the change in texture from skin to something more rubbery.

"Are you this computer speaking to me?"

"Absolutely not. It will only speak to you with answers to questions it can understand. I will speak to you through visions. It is through these visions that we must act together."

"I feel like I'm going crazy."

Willhaven's heart began racing. Then it started relaxing again.

"Did you feel that?"

"Yes, I got tense then relaxed suddenly."

"That is the toy, it tries to normalize everything in you. It prevents over reactions to anything to try and protect you. This constant altering of what should be normal brain activity is what will destroy you."

"Yes, it makes sense. I can't feel any emotion but for a brief moment."

Everything Willhaven felt so far was muted. Even the sensations on the portions of his body that were still flesh felt like some kind of strange numbness.

"The toy had prevented you from dying Willhaven but instead it will kill you slowly and inhumanely."

"Maybe it can be removed?"

"No. The best course of action is we proceed as a team. We will clean this city up for your sake then we will end the program that led to this."

"That program saves people! It's a good program!!" Willhaven was getting excited again but then the brain juices were halted back to normal levels.

That thing had a point. What was it really that was speaking? Was it my subconscious? His mind was racing with thoughts. Could it be the chip malfunctioning? Could he be going insane!?

"Going forward you will receive my divinations as visions. You will act on these. Having success will bring you closer to our goals."

"I want Draco!"

"Yes, I will give you Draco, you will see. Though it seems an impossible feat, it won't be with me by your side. Follow my guidance."

The thought of getting revenge pleased him but the irrationality of thinking he could take down Draco even with all of VARS seemed impossible.

"You must win over Leighwind, take over VARS then we go get Draco. We will handle everyone that impedes our way." The sinister voice said.

"Yes, that is what I want."

Willhaven woke staring at the ceiling. It was only a few hours sleep he received but the dream was vivid. He remembered it well and it gave him hope. Maybe his subconscious was guiding him or maybe he was going crazy.

***

When the next day arrived Willhaven immediately marched to Stephen Kline's office.

"Hello Doctor."

"Hello Will. Please call me Stephen."

"Stephen, I would like a full understanding of the computer in me. Everything."

"Sure. Its actually quite simple and brilliant. It interfaces between you and your prosthetics…"

"Between my brain and my body right!?"

"…Yes…So to speak. I mean it's an interface that allows…"

"I know what you have already told me Stephen. But it's not behaving that way. Everything I feel has a numbness to it or artificial feeling. The skin on my back for example, I do not sense touch how I remember it."

"Interesting. The chip is not supposed to…"

"That chip is also neutralizing my mood constantly. It almost seems like I'm partially lobotomized."

"Don't be over dramatic. It protects you by preventing…"

"Preventing me from getting too stressed, excited, sad or happy Stephen. How else would you describe it."

"I think you just need to get used to it. It may take some time."

"Am I able to control the chip in any way?"

"You can send it signals for muscle movement and ask mathematical questions that it can give you answers to. It scans your brain constantly."

Willhaven was becoming enraged but then he normalized again.

"I see. You are right, I will just need some time."

What has this fool done! I have no autonomy anymore, no privacy anymore. My subconscious is right. The program must be taken over. He thought to himself.

"Thank you, Stephen, for that extra information. I must see Mr. Leighwind."
"Take care Will."

Willhaven made his way to Leighwind's office, but he was not there. His secretary informed Willhaven that Leighwind was very ill and could not come into the office today. Willhaven hastily made his way into a cab and headed for Mr. Leighwind's mansion.

Willhaven arrived in about an hour due to heavy traffic. Once there he was announced and welcomed in. He made his way to Leighwind's bedroom and was greeted with a big smile. Mr. Leighwind had breathing tubes in his nose and was bedridden. His condition had worsened in just about a year. Willhaven began to experience a vision at that moment. In that vision he saw Leighwind on his deathbed. Standing around him was Willhaven himself, Dr. Kline and several others close to him.

"So, his time is very near." Willhaven thought. "I need to move quickly."

"Hello Will how are you feeling."

"Hello Mr. Leighwind. I am fully recovered. I had to see you to express my gratitude for what you and the doctors have done for me."

"Will…It's the least we could have done after your contributions to the program. And the girl you saved she is doing well."

"Yes, Carinne. I am glad to hear that. Mr. Leighwind…I would like a challenge thrown my way. I want you to see my capability, I want to bring this program to its next evolutionary phase."

Mr. Leighwind loved the sound of those words. He was unable to hold back his joy.

"Will, there has been a string of armed robberies lately. One such robbery has cost me several million in physical gold I had stored in the bank that was robbed. With your abilities I'm sure you could investigate and help us get leads and stop the group behind this."

"Mr. Leighwind, I can do much more than that and I would be honored to do this for you."

"Will, don't do anything rash. We have resources here. You don't have to work alone and take risks."

"I plan to use VARS resources, but it would help me greatly if you could expedite the allocations."

"What do you need Will?"

"I want a team of 4 assigned to me. They will aid me."

"I will take care of it immediately."

Willhaven tipped his hat and left. Back at headquarters he handpicked 4 shadows he had previously worked with and began training them. Their training was simple as all they needed to do was create diversions to ease the pressure on him but at no point were they to initiate action. A day later Willhaven found a stack of papers on his desk at VARS containing limited information about the bank heists. He opened one of the manila folders and stared at it. He seemed to leave consciousness, then when he focused again it looked as if the pages had turned themselves and he was midway through the documents. He lost focus again and when he regained it the folders were closed. "Am I **hallucinating** ?" he thought to himself, then he began to have a vision.

The vision presented a newly opened bank; it had vaults in the basement and a large lobby. He saw the perpetrators walking into the bank as a team of 4. There was a giant clock in the center of the bank, the time read 9 am on its large hands. The first two robbers entered individually and the second two entered as a pair. One got on line, and when he arrived at the teller window he pulled out a gun, grabbed a woman behind him waiting on line and threatened to "Blow the bitches head off" if the teller did not cooperate. The second was near one of the security guards and quickly armed himself and took the guard as hostage, disarming him and standing near the entrance. The third grabbed the manager at gunpoint and was escorted down to the vaults along with the fourth. Then Willhaven saw the car out front. A black 1965 Cadillac Fleetwood, it looked new. The vision was done. Willhaven had his marching orders.

"So, that's the scene." Willhaven thought to himself. He moved the Manila folder aside without having looked further at it. He would trust the divination. It's time to equip some battle gear. Willhaven called Dr. Kline and asked him to get a view of the armaments available. They met in the large basement of the VARS building and walked from display case to display case. One case that got Willhaven's attention contained a mechanical appendage that would connect into one of the slots. When activated it would raise much like a 3rd arm and fire large metal darts in all forward and rearward facing directions. Willhaven need only look at his target then think, and the attack would execute. They continued their walk and another device that attracted Willhaven's attention was a mechanical grapple. It functioned as a 3rd arm and could be used for quick navigation in all upward based directions. He considered for a brief moment the value that fast movement would provide in escape and pursuit.

"I will try the dart firing mechanism and the grapple."

"Good choices." Dr. Kline pulled one from the case and handed it to Willhaven.

"All you do Will is bring it near the slot and the CPU will detect it's presence and magnetically attach it."

Willhaven performed the action as instructed and the device

basically attached itself. After a few minutes he understood how to operate it. The mechanical brain in him fed the knowledge. He fired a few test darts into a chair.

"This has excellent penetration. Deadly force." Willhaven said.

They walked back to the display case containing the grapple. Same as before Stephen handed it over and Willhaven attached it immediately. He aimed it upwards to an exposed beam in the ceiling and suspended himself for a moment then pulled himself upward quickly then dropped.

"Fantastic!" Willhaven exclaimed.

Willhaven prepared the team of 4 shadows that would be joining him with their responsibilities. Two of them would enter the bank when it opened at 9 am. One would be near the security guard and another near the teller. It is the one nearest the teller whose job it is to take the place of the hostage Willhaven described from his vision. The other two shadows would remain outdoors near the Cadillac to provide support to Willhaven.

"Remember team, while you are shadows in the employment of VARS, tomorrow you will behave as normal citizens. Have your armor equipped underneath your clothes should anything go unplanned of course."

A collective nod went towards Willhaven.

"For the team in the bank, allow the thieves to get their riches and let them make their way back to the car, when all four of them are in the car, that's when I attack. They will no doubt exit the car immediately. I will need the two of you stationed by the car to be ready to intercept and quickly subdue them. Allow them to exit the car partially then block them in. The two in the front seat will be focused on me. Any questions?"

One of them nodded, another gave a thumbs up one remained silent, and the last one said "Understood!".

Meanwhile Willhaven considered the fact that he would be in the direct line of fire of all four of the robbers. While his body was significantly protected his head and face were not. He made his way back to the VARS basement and took another look around. In another area which contained defensive equipment he found a black duster hat, it had a wide flat brim. It looked very suave, and he could use it to protect his head. He removed his cap and picked up the duster hat. It was heavy, upon closer inspection he observed within the crown there was a metal mask which could be pulled downward to protect the face. He put the hat on, it was a little loose, but he could fix that later by stuffing the rim. He pulled the face mask down which caused a mechanism to simultaneously lower a plate behind his head which dropped down several inches protecting the upper part of the back of his neck. It also acted as a counterbalance to the face mask he was pulling down which protected his eyes and his nose. The mask had a ghastly look when deployed. The metal face had prominent cheeks, and the eyelets had a dark yellow lens in each that when in low light would amplify all ambient light sources. Willhaven turned off the lights to test it and sure enough, any light in the dim room was amplified. Beneath the nose portion of the mask which covered only down to Willhaven's upper lip it formed a row of teeth, the effect of which was clearly meant to induce psychological fear in all opponents facing it.

"This will do!" He thought as he turned and left.

***

The next day arrived quickly. Willhaven was in his spot which he claimed late the following night. He got little sleep and prepared his spot by obscuring it further by breaking off branches from higher up in the tree and making a makeshift nest where he would hide, this would obscure him from view from anyone below looking up, should that happen. In front of the bank a large tree stood which was where Willhaven made his nest. He sat there perched waiting patiently. As time rolled on and morning arrived, he saw one of the shadows take a position and lean up against the bank. He began reading the morning paper to blend in. Willhaven then saw the second shadow across the street. He pulled out a cigar and began smoking while staring in the direction of traffic. Time was almost at hand. A blue

Mustang pulled up into the spot where the Cadillac was expected.

"Interesting. Let's see what happens." Willhaven thought.

The line began forming and he saw the other two shadows on line completing the arrival of his team. The troops are all deployed and at their stations. Excellent. Down below Willhaven spotted the black Cadillac as it pulls up alongside the blue Mustang. Willhaven smiled for a moment then focused again on the scene below. An argument ensued over the spot and the Mustang was forced to move on.

"And so, it begins!" Willhaven thought as he prepared himself. One thug exited the car first and got to the line. Then a moment later a second thug exited the car and found a spot on the line. As the bank opened and let people in the other two exited the car and now made their way in to join the rest of their crew. The driver who had remained in place stepped out and opened the trunk of the car just ever so slightly then hopped back into the driver's seat. Everything was quiet from Willhaven's perch. Everything was serene in fact. A lovely sunny day, birds singing, you would think that nothing could break this mood. As the minutes moved on the driver, who remained in the car, started the engine. Probably about twenty minutes had passed when the burglars ejected themselves from the bank stampeding towards their car. The trunk was already loose as they expected, and they plopped their full sacks within it and slammed it shut. Three were in the car when it started to pull away. The fourth was trying to get into the rear passenger side but was getting pulled away with the car.

"Damn it. Has to be now." Then at this point Willhaven dropped from the tree parting the makeshift nest as he fell. He landed on the hood of the car, his weight collapsing in the left side. He immediately leaned over and peeled back the right side as if it were tin foil, it was already bent somewhat due to the fall impact. Willhaven then reached in and ripped out the battery wire. The burglar that was still making his way into the rear passenger seat of the car stopped midway in and began to reach for his gun but was tackled by Willhaven's guard, the shadow that was reading the paper earlier. From the rear passenger side facing the street the door was thrown open and a thug began to jump out but before he could fully extract himself he was tackled by Willhaven's other guard who darted across the street to join the fray. While this was happening, the driver reached out his window with his gun pointed at Willhaven, he managed to fire one shot but Willhaven's artificially intelligent chip intervened on his behalf and with his mechanical hand deflected the projectile elsewhere. Willhaven then punched through the windshield reaching down towards the ignition and turned off the car. He then removed the keys which he dropped immediately and ripped the steering column out. From over his shoulder

Willhaven heard his name called:

"Will They killed him! They fucking killed him!"

The hostage…They killed the hostage he realized. It was unexpected but no time to consider it now Willhaven thought. The announcement had caused excitement in Willhaven which was quickly subdued by his computerized companion. In this instance it was a welcome action as it allowed his focus to remain trained on his targets.

"Do it Will, make them pay!" The voice was so clear he almost looked around thinking it had come from someone nearby--but no--it was in his head, and he agreed with it. He dove his body partially in through the broken windshield using his arms to lift the roof of the car pushing it upwards enough to accommodate him. He further peeled the windshield away, separating it from the car body and pressed it into the front seat. Willhaven then peeled the debris away from the driver's side giving him easy reach which he used to crush the drivers head in using both hands, it cracked and brain matter oozed out from between his mechanical fingers. The passenger moved enough of the windshield debris away to have more movement and an unobstructed area and began firing and as he did so Willhaven pulled himself back out of the car causing the bullets to ricochet off of his chest armor. He jumped on the hood. The two thugs in the rear were disarmed and pinned on the ground at this point.

With the driver dead two remained in the front seat flailing. Immediately Willhaven grabbed the front passenger door edge and dented it, breaking the window. The dent prevented the door from opening. He then ripped a portion of the roof away as if he were peeling a banana and slammed his pointer finger down into one thug's skull so forcefully that it deformed and partially collapsed it in. Willhaven then disarmed the last one, pulled him out of the car, quickly tied him up and jumped back into the trees. Nearly all of the crowd that formed stayed at a distance. A few brave on lookers ran out to assist the three shadows in keeping the thugs subdued. Willhaven jumped from one tree to the next until he was out of view. He had made his way into a nearby park covered in bush and trees and descended then made his way on to an isolated path then back on to a quiet neighborhood street, perfectly calm, walking back to VARS as discreetly as his large frame would allow. His hands were wiped clean of the blood but remained concealed none-the-less. The grapple, he observed, was not needed as he was able to jump great distances and his mechanical arms were strong enough to grab any surface.

The next day the headlines in the newspapers reported on a masked hero stepping in to stop a burglary in action aided by some brave bystanders. The three shadows that survived were interviewed by Geoff Bryson, a local reporter who thought they were ordinary citizens just minding their own business. They intentionally gave conflicting descriptions of Willhaven, but all three stating that the individual aiding them did not wear any mask. The only photograph of Willhaven was taken by a bystander about 50 feet away. It was during his departure and though it had his full profile in it the armored mask caused the image in the photograph to appear to have a deformed face which could barely be made out due to the blur the motion caused.

Meanwhile Terrance Leighwind had heard the news and was both impressed with Willhaven's ability to have caught them, which also led to his gold being discovered and returned, but also dismayed at the loss of one of their own. The bittersweet victory ultimately did not present Willhaven in a negative light to Terrance. It did not matter to him about their level of training, only the outcome and the cost was paid. When Willhaven returned to his room he thought about what had gone wrong. The vision was wrong! Was the first assumption.

He replayed the vision in his mind remembering many of the fine details. He closed his eyes to focus on it.

He again observes the newly opened bank, it had vaults in its basement and a large lobby. He saw the perpetrators walking into the bank as a staggered team of 4. There was a giant clock in the center of the bank, the time read 9 am on its large hands. The first two robbers entered individually and the second two entered as a pair. One got on line then when he was at the teller pulled out a gun, grabbed a woman behind him waiting on line and threatened to "Blow the bitches head off" if the teller did not cooperate.

At this point in his recollection, he made a realization. He opened his eyes in shock! He realized he had changed the vision when he ordered one of the shadows to take the place of the original hostage, the woman!! In his eagerness to save a life, which he did, he exchanged it for one of his own team members.

"I understand now what happened." He said to himself. He asked his artificially intelligent brain about alternatives that could have led to all surviving but the options it offered required breaking the law. That is to say, apprehending the criminals before any crime could be committed, before they even entered the bank. He was not able to be overcome by any feelings good or bad for very long. Though he experienced them briefly and powerfully, it was only a passing moment as his neurological senses were reset to neutral. He shifted his thoughts elsewhere as he wrote the situation off as a success. He thought about his interactions with the thugs and where he may have had some limits. He also was beginning to realize that he would not need the dart attachment either. The fact that he was able to deflect a bullet with his hand meant that he could carry darts instead and throw them with perfect accuracy thereby freeing a slot for a better attachment. He hastened back to Dr. Kline, to take another look at the armaments

VARS had developed. Back at the VARS headquarters both Willhaven and Dr. Kline discussed the options.

"This is all we have Will. What did you have in mind?"

Willhaven thought to himself for a couple of minutes then the idea came to him or perhaps was given to him.

"I would like another set of arms, but I have some enhancements I would like added!"

"It will take some time to develop but let's head up to the lab and document your requirements. We can see if it's within our capabilities."

The ability Willhaven desired was to deal with a crowd of thugs. His first downfall was being overpowered. He was not prepared for it, and he would be damned if he would make the same mistake twice. If he had another set of arms, the bank incident would most likely have gone differently. Yes, he thought! He would not have needed any shadows with him; he could have taken them all on his own. More violence would have been needed but no innocent lives would have been lost.

This is what must be done. His mind began racing with what enhancements he would add, oh the possibilities! Several days had passed and late one evening Willhaven came down with fever. He had retired to his room at VARS dorms early that day but could not sleep. He had not been able to sleep well since his final operation, but he could at least pass out for several hours which had sufficed. Tonight, however there was an infection running rampant. He thought it might be his body rejecting his bionics. He tossed and turned. The CPU in his body did not have programming to deal with this situation yet, however it kept trying to control his brain. It attempted to "normalize" chemical responses which would normally signal his body to attack the virus.

"Spirit, can you hear me?" Willhaven called out in his mind.

"Spirit…Are you there…Can you hear me?" He called out through his voice box.

"I think I am dying."

A reply came in the form of a vision. The vision was hard to receive due to the pain and discomfort Willhaven was already fighting. His fever was ramping up. The vision showed him standing over his own body on a dark roof top. He was sitting but slumped forward. Then a moment later he was ground level. There were black birds all around him. Very large black birds, he recognized them, they were ravens. He began walking and they parted out of his way revealing a path that led towards a bright light. He stepped into it and was on the other side. It looked like paradise. In front of him he saw another version of himself. This version of him was fully human. This other version of him walked up to a rose. The rose had a visible aura to it. As he stood and watched he saw his clone then trace a strange shape in front of it. As his finger passed through the air it left a momentary red translucent trace line behind it, a final form appearing like a strange rune that may have been a letter or word in an ancient language. After it dissipated the rose began to wither and die. This other version of himself then grabbed a chicken out of a nearby bush. He saw his clone close his eyes then he pet the chicken once, placed it gently on the ground calming it, then making a V shape with both hands, palms face up, gently tapped the bird. He then opened his eyes, turned to face Willhaven so that he was staring at himself. He noticed black spots all over his clone which began disappearing. The chicken then fell dead behind him. The vision then ended.

Willhaven woke immediately at this point covered in sweat.

"I think I know what I need to do!" He thought as he ran outside.

He moved quickly looking around then saw a raccoon jumping out of a trash can. He leaped over to it before it could register that he was there and he grabbed it. He slammed the back of its head with the back of one of his metal hands to knock it unconscious then he lay the animal gently on the ground. He closed his eyes and thought for a moment about death, then made the V formation from his vision and pressed his hands against the raccoon gently. Nothing happened and his fever was getting worse fast. His vision was now blurry, and he felt faint. He closed his eyes again and with a suggestion that had just been fed to him he said to himself:

"You will die!" He pressed against the raccoon again.

At first it seemed like nothing happened but then the raccoon stopped breathing. Willhaven began feeling better almost immediately. The fever had broken and while the sweat remained, he had recovered. He had passed death on to another.

"What kind of terrible skill is this!"

Then he said out loud.

"It is not my time." And he was taken aback not expecting to have uttered those words.

On his way back to his bedroom he came across an orchid in the lobby, he decided to do the motions he saw in the vision. He traced the strange runic shape as he remembered it and the plant began to wither and die.

"I know what that is now." He thought to himself. His otherworldly knowledge was coming to him. He would have more visions and learn more runic motions before this night would end.

***

The following day Willhaven went to visit Dr. Kline. He was walking up to Stephen Kline's home, a quaint Tudor home that today would bear witness to an extraordinary exchange. Willhaven knocked and was admitted in. They both sat and Willhaven began the conversation:

"Dr. Kline..."

"Will, you can call me Stephen." He interrupted.

"Stephen, I am here to discuss this computer in me. It has a severe malfunction. One of many I have come to discover and one last night that almost cost me my life."

"Oh my GOD Will! Are you alright? what happened?"

"I had a fever which kept worsening. I could feel my body trying to do something, I had some tremors, the CPU it seems could not handle the situation. I felt a war occurring in my head, a rush of emotions followed by desertion of all emotion. I felt like I was going to die Stephen."

"The chip is programmed to protect you..."

Willhaven cut him off.

"It is programmed to calm me or give me adrenaline when needed but when I was sick it did not know what to do and it was blocking my brain's normal responses. I was dying, this was certain to me."

The tone caught Dr. Kline off guard, perhaps the chip was indeed malfunctioning he thought. He should not be showing this much emotion. He could see then that Willhaven calmed back down and he dismissed it as a temporary slowness in processing. "I think you may be over dramatizing Will."

"Stephen, you need to end your research and your portion of the VARS program."

"I'm sorry to inform you that's not gonna happen."

"I see."

"We are having success, and I've spent my life creating this beautiful machine that has saved you."

If Willhaven could get angry and stay that way this would be the moment where he would become temporarily insane but unfortunately his hell is to be stoic. The problem with this neutrality of mood, he observed, was that everyone he dealt with did not comprehend the true nature of the situation such as Stephen Kline. His dismissiveness right now was proof of this. Words without emphasis do not carry enough weight. Willhaven decided to adjust his wording hoping for more success but also another thought had just occurred to him to ensure the program is ended.

"Let me explain something to you Stephen."

Willhaven stood up and looked down on Stephen. He raised a hand as he began speaking.

He placed his hand on Stephen's chest just below Stephen's right nipple and he spoke thusly:

"Nature gave man sentience and rationality at this point." Willhaven pressed his finger gently on Stephen. He then slid his finger across Stephen's chest to the center and spoke again:

"Man thinks he mastered sentience and rationality at this point, but he has not and is only a tinkerer, but a dangerous one."

Then Willhaven slid his finger down about five inches to just above the belly button and spoke again:

"Man makes creations to control man's sentience and rationality at this point and thinks he has succeeded."

Willhaven then moved his finger upwards to just below the other nipple and spoke again:

"Man inflicts sentience and rationality onto man in the name of man to save man at this point."

Willhaven makes one final trace back directly down about five inches and spoke again:

"Man discovers a truth that places man on the path of the GODS at this point which man is not ready for."

Willhaven finished his story, finished placing a death mark on Stephen and hoped that Stephen got the message. If so, he would remove the mark. Throughout the entire scenario Stephen had stared back and forth between Willhaven and his finger motions in puzzlement. At the end however, he felt a strange cold feeling come over him that he could not explain.

"Willhaven, please leave now."

"Goodbye Doctor." Willhaven did not tip his hat and left immediately.

***

In the following months Willhaven performed flawlessly for VARS. Leighwind was elated at the sudden and expeditious progress Willhaven had brought. It was time, however, to make the request—no, demand—Willhaven thought to himself. Visions had been guiding Willhaven and would continue but there was one important one that now revealed itself as being due. Willhaven made his way to Leighwind's mansion and was welcomed in. Willhaven knew Leighwind's time was short which drove him to work harder and faster at impressing him. Through his visions he knew what the outcome would be, and he would take all precautions should he have misinterpreted anything. Willhaven was escorted to Mr. Leighwind's bedroom where he spent most of his days now.

"Hello Mr. Leighwind. I am pleased to see you. I hope that I have not disturbed you to badly but there is an urgent matter I think we need to discuss."

"Hello Will." Mr. Leighwind was straining to speak. He was pleased to see Willhaven, as he managed to smile.

"What is on your mind."

"The future of VARS concerns me. Who will be in charge after you?"

"Will, I have given this much thought. I thought about everything you have given and continue to give, believe me. But I was thinking of putting Stephen Kline in charge and you would report directly to him. There is always a place for you here."

"I see Mr. Leighwind. I do respect your wishes, but you should know that I have been having discussions with Dr. Kline about his inventions and their shortcomings."

"Will, what… what do you mean? They saved your life."

"Mr. Leighwind, with all due respect, my life has not been saved. I am being tortured daily by this hardware and software. I cannot feel emotions but for a fleeting moment. If I get happy this chip subdues the experience, if I get angry this chip subdues the experience, I have never experienced much fear but now I experience none. In the recent past I used fear as a tool to judge the severity of a situation whereas now it's simply a mathematical evaluation that is either true or false and it doesn't even feel like that calculation is happening at all. I am forced into stoicism of the most extreme manner. Several months back I had a fever that almost killed me because this chip cannot stop itself from interfering with my brain functions. I was led to believe this only received brain input and did not provide or alter brain activity. It is mis programmed, and it will kill anyone else who receives this. Mr. Kline, the good Doctor, will not listen to me. I am hoping that you can understand this Mr. Leighwind. It is very serious."

"I..I don't know what to say Will."

"Give me control. Of everything. I can fix it all."

"Oh I…I don't know. I mean I've known Stephen for many years."

"This is unfortunate Mr. Leighwind. Very very unfortunate for you…"

"Will, that sounds very menacing."

"Mr. Leighwind, your wife once told you that the Leighwind

name should be remembered honorably and associated with saving lives did she not."

"Yes, yes she did but how did you know that!"

"There is another side effect of my circumstances that I have not mentioned to anyone yet. I am going to mention it to you because we have little time to make a correction. Terrance, this affects your soul and your family name. When I recovered from my operation I had died as I'm sure you had been made aware. When I returned, I did not return alone. There is a death spirit guiding me setting things correctly. It has brought me messages from your deceased family and other divinations. This may sound ludicrous but let me dispel all doubts right now by telling you that on your wife's death bed she whispered the words "I'm afraid" into your ears."

"No, no, no no no it can't be."

"Terrance, death is with you in this room right now. You have a simple decision to make to save your soul and your family name. Make me the final and full heir to VARS."

"I…I..Can't. Will, I have to…."

Willhaven saw his blood pressure rising, his vitals were getting dangerous and he started to have a heart attack. Alarm beeps went off summoning nurses which ran in. Terrance was grasping his chest while looking at Willhaven. Willhaven then calmly raised an arm amongst the ruckus and as he waved it over Terrance he said:

"It's not your time yet."

All vitals returned to normal, and all pain left Terrance. He was able to think clearly for the first time in months.

"I think the nurses can leave now, right?" Willhaven said demandingly.

"Nurses, please leave us. I'm ok now." Leighwind confirmed.

They left with a puzzled look on their faces.

"Please, please don't kill me."

"I cannot do anything to stop what's coming Terrance, but I can make you this promise. I can make your exit from this life completely painless to you in exchange for control of VARS. You need not worry about your name; I will protect the program as long as I live and your name will be remembered fondly."

Terrance thought about the offer. He was already including Willhaven in his will so this would be a small shift of the pen to correct. The thought of a painless end to what was pain ridden years filled him with hope. He wanted more reassurance however.

"I will do as you ask but I would like it to be painless from this moment to the end."

"Done." Willhaven replied with reassuring sternness.

"Willhaven closed his eyes, and his mind began beckoning the spirit within to oblige."

He opened his eyes and stared at Terrance.

"I…I can feel it. I feel much better!"

Willhaven nodded then turned to leave. Terrence Leighwind then decided to remove the oxygen hoses from his nose and discovered he was able to breathe with ease again. A feeling so welcome to him that he closed his eyes for a moment and took deep unrestrained breaths. He then looked over at Willhaven.

"Thank you Will." He heard it as he was leaving causing him to stop for just a moment before moving on. He did not turn to look at Terrence but simply continued on his way. He would visit Terrance daily afterwards for several days. On the fourth day Terrance confirmed the agreement had been honored on his end leaving everything to Willhaven and on the fifth visit Willhaven guided Terrance into a deep sleep from which all vitals flat lined. Terrence Leighwind III died peacefully in his sleep as promised. The last dream he had was also not interrupted. It was a dream where he had walked into a splendid garden adorned throughout with vine trellises and flowers. At the end was a fountain where he met with his wife.

The news of the full transfer of ownership had made its way to Stephen Kline who was exceedingly upset and driven to destroy his office at the VARS headquarters. Stephen received a sum of about 5 million dollars which did nothing to stave off his rage. Terrance had never mentioned this to him even as he stood by on his death bed alongside Willhaven who had been behaving strangely to Stephen. He began to wonder about his chip.

***

Several months had passed and Willhaven decided to reach out to Carinne. The records at VARS show that she remained in Hope City and is under the employment of VARS as one of its shadow warriors.

He pulled her current address and decided to take stewardship of her employment and training.

Later that day there was a knock at her door. Carinne turned quickly with a surprised look on her face, wide eyed. She hustled over to the door and looked through the peephole. She was only able to see someone's chest, broad and vast.

"Just a minute!" She ran towards the closet and grabbed a knife which she placed in a sheath then tucked under her shirt. "Who's there?" She asked through the closed door.

"Willhaven. I would like to speak with you."

The voice box sound caught her off guard.

She unlocked the door and let him in. They both sat opposite each other at the kitchen table. Willhaven began the conversation with the announcement.

"Carinne, I stopped by personally to see how you were doing but also to let you know that I have moved your stewardship in VARS to report directly to me."

"Oh, I see. Thank you for checking in. I'm doing ok."

"Carinne, we spoke briefly after my operations, I had asked you to leave Hope City for your safety. I am disappointed to see that you are still here."

"I'm sorry Will, I know. I said I would leave but I can't just yet."

"I expected that response. I would like to train you in self-defense Carinne. While Draco has moved on to other things it's always possible he can come back looking for you. This training will be essential not just for anything that may challenge you here but elsewhere."

"I look forward to it Will."

He reached out and grabbed her hands and held them. She felt the cold metal as they gently held her fingers.

"I will take care of Draco. He will pay for what he did to your family and what he did to me Carinne."

"Will, are you doing ok?" She heard about the torture Willhaven had endured but the sight and feel of his new mechanical hands made the cold truth evident.

"We are all suffering in our own way Carinne. I have always been nearly immune to pain and fear. Probably that led me to this outcome but also equally probable is that I would be dead. I am going to use this new body and mind to clean up this city. I have something big planned that I'm working on. It will also address Draco and the corrupt mayor he is working to install. I am asking many of our shadows to leave Hope City, to start a new life elsewhere. This goes double for you Carinne. I will take care of Draco on your behalf. You cannot do it alone and even with a team there is a very high risk of death for you."

"But Will, the danger is there for you as well, we should work together!"

"NO! You are not aware of my abilities, I can take Draco down, but I need you and the others that are under protection to embrace your new lives, to rebuild elsewhere. Fight crime in your own ways suitable to your capabilities but not directly if possible. What you are attempting to do is very personal and up close. That is too dangerous. I don't expect to convince you easily, but I want you to always think about this. Think about tomorrow."

"Thank you Will, I do appreciate your concern."

"There is one more thing I want to show you."

Willhaven removed his upper coat and revealed a second set of arms. This set had large forearms that appeared to contain other components within and had separation lines as if they could expand to reveal some other capability if needed.

"Oh my GOD Will! What happened to you!!" She released his hands and recoiled in shock.

"This is what has become of me. When I saved you that night I was overtaken by Draco's men. He sent quite a few of them to kidnap, then torture and kill you. They wanted the information your brother gave you. We took that, hid you and I managed to kill a few of them but I was overcome when more arrived. I went through an operation to save my life."

Willhaven stood up and placed a foot on the chair.

"Look Carinne, they destroyed my arms and legs. All these prosthetics are weapons. Besides giving me movement they give me strength and abilities to deal with multiple assailants simultaneously. I am also heavily armored."

He opened his under coat and exposed his shirt. His armor's outline could be seen printing on it.

"So this should ease your mind when I tell you I am more than ready to take on Draco. But even with these enhancements I will not take him on directly if it's not necessary. I have a plan I am putting in place that will succeed. I am fully confident of it. For this plan to work however I need you and the other shadows to leave Hope City. If you do not start your new lives and forget this place, I cannot consider you saved. I say this earnestly, leave and start a new life. I have this under control; I have a computer implanted in me that is also performing calculations which aids me in quick thinking. Rest easy. His time is coming. If you feel up to it, we can start your training tomorrow."

"Ok Will, tomorrow will work." The thought of becoming dangerous was appealing to Carinne. She heard Willhaven's message, but her heart had other plans. She looked Willhaven over with sadness. He laid out a schedule which she confirmed and when her training would begin. It would last about a year after which she was to continue practice on her own then leave Hope City. She did not however. Another year fell off the calendar, Willhaven waited several months and when he checked her status again, she was still in Hope City. Four more years would pass with the invisible chains binding her there. By now however, Willhaven's plan was nearly ready to implement. As he began making plans to pay her another visit, he learned from one of the shadows that reported to him that she was planning an attack on the mayor during a speech he would give at his town hall meeting. Willhaven immediately called Carinne to prevent any unnecessary deaths or escalations. Worse still she could expose the shadows through reckless actions.

The phone rang in the kitchen. Carinne had just finished some exercises. She was excited about the event she had planned with a couple of shadows she would team up with to pull it off. She wiped sweat from her face as she grabbed the phone.
"Hello, this is Carinne."

"This is Willhaven."

"Hello Will, we have not spoken in a while. How are you."

"I am concerned. I heard you were planning something at the next town hall. I wanted to discuss this with you."

Carinne twirled the phone cord in her hand with a bit of nervousness.

"Yes, Will. I am planning to kill the mayor. You know how many deaths he is responsible for and that he is working hand in hand with Draco."

"I am well aware. You are not to directly engage with him. That is an order. It's too dangerous and it could expose the shadows. It could even get you and your whole team killed!"

"Will, you know when we join, we know that death is a possibility."

"The point of our death clause to make the signer aware that death is a possibility, however the cause of death should only be due to uncontrollable circumstances. This situation is one you are creating, and the probability of death is 100% for you and your team. I have calculated this. I have also spoken with one of the shadows on your team and expressed the same. We are not to throw our lives away on small gains. Maybe you can succeed in your goal but then what? Draco still lives and will install another corrupt puppet. You die, your team dies, you possibly expose the shadows and VARS as being connected and the change you sought is for nothing or worse. That is a total loss. I forbid you from the action you have planned."

"Will we have to do something we can't just…."

Willhaven had an idea, one that might appease the demons in Carinne but also advance the cause. He interrupted her with a new proposal, one that would prevent her premature death which it seemed she was getting all to comfortable welcoming recently. It's not her time he thought.

"I have an idea Carinne, there is something you can do that

would help. It's also a better way to handle this situation. Proceed extra cautiously with your mission but make the goal to deliver a message. Maybe the mayor can be persuaded to turn himself in and implicate Draco (the thought was comical to Willhaven so much so that a laugh almost escaped his chip's notice). Lenient sentences have been given to political figures that have done this in the past."

Carinne was quiet while she considered the change in plan. Ultimately, she could not argue against Willhaven's facts. There was a high probability of failure if the goal was an assassination. The way he phrased it was 100% failure, she reconsidered. The suicidal part of her subsided for the moment. She had been teasing death, more so in recent months and it seems Willhaven was picking up on it.

***

The clang of metal echoed throughout the wooded area. Birds leapt out of bushes into the air at the sound. The hammer landed violently on the red-hot iron rod. Each beat infused with rage. The metallic clang of each strike echoed from the back of the cabin and out through the double barn doors into the desolate woods. A small pile of flat rectangular steel plates sat by the anvil in a bucket, unformed templates ready to be molded into a tool for revenge. The cabin was recessed in a wooded area about one hundred feet from an isolated road. It was not visible to any passersby and the driveway was made of loose gravel. The front of the cabin had a large kitchen and living area connected by a hallway that led you to the back. Along the way there was a bathroom, a small bedroom and the workshop area. The floor of the workshop is concrete with an edge of about four feet wide running around the workshop which framed in a center section made up of gravel about a foot deep. Another strike sent the metallic clang through the cabin as the object begins to take form. Carinne's blonde hair flows down the back of her head tied and tucked behind a blacksmith's apron. She placed the workpiece back into the kiln for another heat cycle then after some time resumes the hammering. A beveled edge has been formed on one side. The beginnings of a sword shape come into view as she puts it back in the kiln for more heating before the next round of strikes. On a table nearby there are 6 throwing knives laid out. The handles are wrapped in either red or green dyed leather. Red indicates they are or will be tipped with a deadly poison and green will be tipped or coated with a neutralizer. Moving across we see homemade pepper spray grenades which are smaller than actual grenades and two butterfly swords which are about 14" long, also homemade. I'm ready she thought. Here I come Frank.

***

3 days later a figure, unseen by anyone and protected by the

cover of night, is perched on a rooftop looking down on City Hall. One of the oldest buildings in Hope City. A city which is in the process of expanding outward faster than it is upward. Its architecture is mostly Gothic and accounts for a good portion of the city. Its skyline is scratched by a newly constructed bank towering at thirty floors. The city sits nestled at the bottom of a valley surrounded by mountains. Beyond the city limits a slow rise in elevation occurs with a popular hangout spot being a high ridge looking down upon it. The static lights from the buildings mixed in with the flowing movement of headlights and taillights gives off an impression of some type of ethereal body, the moving traffic it's blood flow.

The figure leaves its perch and runs across the rooftop lit by the night sky, drops down to another rooftop below, then sprints over to the next. Gargoyle statues guide the way while decorating and protecting the structures from evil. The figure eventually drops into a tree then climbs over to the City Hall rooftop. The Town Hall meeting begins allowing people in and the figure is perched high above looking down on the crowd and out into the distance checking for any new signals from a lookout being communicated by an arm gesture that would call off the plan if anything became too risky to proceed. Luckily no sign came. The long line starts dwindling as people make their way into the main conference area. The seating allowed for all that were waiting on line with a small number of seats left open.

The cold evening air greeted the crowd as the 8 pm start time arrived. In attendance was Geoff Bryson, a reporter for the Hope City Daily. Geoff was average height at about 5'10 with dark features. He had straight black hair and very dark brown eyes. His light complexion and slender build would make someone who didn't know him think he was in a rock band. Geoff started recording on the video camera then turned over to his assistant.

"Hey Beth." He looked over and noticed she was writing notes on her flip pad.

"Hey Beth." He tapped her on her arm this time to get her attention.

"Oh, yea sorry let me start the recorder."

"It's good to have if anything were to go wrong with the video recording. I like having a backup of some kind." Geoff said.

"Yea, we should be all set for a boring two hours."

"Yea I know, same shit, he will lower the cost of living, fight crime and improve the city's economy."

"Yea." Beth said through a yawn watching the stage with a blank stare.

"Hopefully this goes by fast." Geoff also fought off a yawn.

Meanwhile up on stage the mayor stood and walked over to the podium. He was tall and in his mid-forties with black hair and brown eyes. He was heavy set with a slight hunchback.

"Good evening, everyone, this is your Mayor, Frank Lombardi. Welcome to tonight's town hall".

The meeting commenced and the audience silenced themselves. As Frank shuffled his weight standing at the podium the floorboards of the old building creaked into the microphone under his large frame. Frank had been speaking for about 15 minutes and Geoff was looking around at random parts of the auditorium. At one point he randomly looked up and in between the low hanging drop lights, he thought he saw something or someone moving but the movement stopped or maybe it was in his head. He stopped looking at the lights, though dim, they were annoying to look at directly and whatever was above them could not be seen well anyway. Above the lights cloaked in darkness Carinne was looking down on Geoff. She had stopped her movement to get a closer look at him. He was very attractive to her, and she lost her focus for that moment. When her stare met Geoff's wandering eyes, she thought she had been caught but then he looked away. She regained her focus and continued her mission. As the meeting progressed people within the crowd could be seen fiddling, reading or staring at the floor. What everyone was waiting for was the question-and-answer period. The point at which they could pummel Frank with hard questions and watch him squirm. His message fell largely on deaf ears. It was just another well packaged bundle of lies and catch phrases. After about a half hour the lights suddenly went out. A collective gasp could be heard in the audience. The moonlight was double obscured, first by cloud cover and second by the frosted windows used in the auditorium.

"The camera is still recording but it's on battery, what about the audio?" Geoff asked.

"No, it's off. It doesn't run on battery."

"Ok, the camera's audio will have to do but they may cancel if they can't get it working."

There is a bustle as some staffers begin running around. Flashlights can be seen as security walks by speedily trying to isolate the issue.

"Everybody remain calm, we will have this all fixed very soon." Frank called into the crowd as loud as he could with his voice, he was still positioned behind the podium.

The sound of metal cans hitting the floor could be heard scattered throughout the edges of the crowd. Clank, clank, clink sounds were heard right by Geoff's aisle. Smoke begins to erupt from the cans. People begin coughing, then become sleepy, some begin to slump over while others collapse to the floor.

"Beth cover your mouth and let's try to find an exit quick!"
Geoff coughed out the words as his eyes began to water.

He received no response from her however. Feeling around in the
darkness and smoke he found Beth slumped over in her chair.
Immediately he turns and begins feeling his way out of his row
with one hand while using the other to cover his nose and mouth
with the top part of his trench coat only taking breaths as needed.
Geoff was quickly making his way to where he remembered the
nearest exit was but unfortunately drops to his knees and begins
crawling slowly. His vision becoming very blurry and his senses
dulled before passing out just a few feet from the exit. Up on
stage the mayor is being rushed out the doors behind the stage
and down the hall to an available office. Police begin guarding
the entrance and exits to City Hall, being careful to stay out of
the range of the gas. As the Mayor entered the office the officer
escorting him closed the doors.

"We should stay in here Sir we…." He was interrupted by a body
collapsing behind the door he had just closed, he turned his head
back in the direction of the sound. The officer could see gas
seeping in between the door's edges but the cannisters are now
all spent and no further gas would enter.

Frank attempts to use the phone but the lines have been cut along
with the power. Both Frank and the officer hear rustling in the
hallway which is then followed by the door's knob being turned.

The officer seeing this runs to the door and grabs the handle seizing the movement which is immediately followed by a sword stabbing through the top part of the doorway. The officer releases the knob then falls, grabs his gun and fires several rounds through the door. On the other side and hanging upside down Carinne grabs the partially opened door and resumes opening it. More shots are fired through the door in the same spot and now with the door fully opened a dart flies toward the officer sitting on the floor and hits him in the upper leg. He drops his gun and grabs his leg as drowsiness blurs his vision. As he begins to slump over, he sees a dark figure in the hallway dropping to its feet.

"Who's there!" Frank calls out but in the darkness all he can see is the silhouette of a person. He runs behind a desk to take cover but the figure at the doorway raises a compact compound crossbow gun and fires a bolt directly in front of Frank's face impaling itself on the wall. He could feel the wind from it passing. The assailant fought the urge not to kill, that action was forbidden. Revenge would need to wait for the larger plan to unfold. The figure quickly pulled another arrow and loaded it.

"What do you want?" he called out to the masked figure.

The second bolt was fired in response. This one lands in Frank's lower leg. The shadow disappears back into the hallway and the situation ends as quickly as it began. Frank begins to pull the bolt out through grunts and screams as it slides out slowly. On the bolt shaft Frank remove's a note that was wrapped around it.

The note reads:

"Dear Mayor, consider this a warning. You will not seek re-election. You will surrender to the authorities immediately and confess to your connections with the mob and the assassinations you have conspired in throughout your career. Fail to do this and you will be removed by deadly force if necessary."

The note is signed by DAVID BENSON.

David Benson is dead for sure; Frank knew the name. It was his first victim. Framed and murdered by Frank and Draco for getting too close to exposing the truth about him. Anger replaced the pain in his leg as he crumpled the note and put it in his pocket. In the hallway he hears footsteps running toward him, two more officers heading his way, one stops to assist the officers on floor knocked out by the gas which has now subsided, and the other officer makes his way to assist Frank.

"Sir, are you ok?"

"NO, I'VE BEEN SHOT WITH AN ARROW! IT HURTS LIKE HELL!"

"Did you see who did it sir?"

"I couldn't make them out; they never stepped in from the hallway."

Just then the lights are restored.

***

The following day investigators arrived and began to comb through the crime scene. They could always be spotted because they dressed the same way. Long heavy coats, vests and felt hats. The lead investigator, Detective Patrick Warn looks over the office Frank was attacked in for any extra clues. He was of average height with a slender build and youthful looking even though he was in his early forties. His blue eyes were always narrow as he seemed to always be lost in thought. He wore a black fedora above a full head of red hair which he often tilted back during investigations exposing more of his forehead.

"Mark, are you done getting fingerprints?"

Mark looked over with a cold glance "Yes Mr. Warn." Mark was just an inch shorter than Patrick and on the heavier side. He had brown hair, brown eyes and wore a light-colored fedora.

"Any clues about what happened?"

"We know the assailant was in the building prior to the session beginning but they were not captured on any cameras due to the lighting going out. No one was harmed except for the mayor."

"Was there any other evidence besides the gas cannisters, darts and bolts?"

"We haven't found anything else yet. It does appear though that they picked the locks as no evidence was found of forced entry."

Two additional officers now enter the room escorting Mayor Frank Lombardi.

"Well well if it isn't our finest detective, Mr. Patrick Warn!" Frank said in a welcoming tone.

"Hello Mr Lombardi, I hope you are feeling better now." Pat replied in a neutral tone.

"My leg is ok, I have a slight limp, but I'm told it will heal in a couple of weeks. Thankfully the assassin had bad aim."

"Well, I would not go that far." Pat replied.

"No?"

"The bolts we recovered had bullet type heads. These are not deadly and used for target practice mainly and a leg shot would not be life threatening in many cases involving bolts such as these."

"Interesting." Frank lost his smile and furled his forehead.

"If this person wanted you dead you would be. The first bolt is at eye level and was embedded in the wall behind this desk. I think this was the first shot and likely just to stop you from hiding or reaching for a gun." Pat pointed to the hole in the wall left by the arrow.

"Go on." Frank stated.

"The bolt that landed in your leg was intentional and we know the assailant has excellent aim. I examined both bolts and they are not the same. One has green fletching, and one has red fletching." Pat replied.

"I don't know what if anything that means yet." Pat continued.

"What's a fletching?" Frank asked.

"It's the feathering on the back of the bolt that guides it through the air."

"Ah I see." Frank replied, scratching his chin.

"Did you have any interaction with them at all? Did they say anything? Any type of communication?" Pat asked.

"No nothing."

"Maybe they left some clues we missed." Patrick walked out with Mark to investigate the other areas of the building. Later in the day a phone rings at the other end of Hope City.

"Hello, Amichi residence how may I help you?" The butler answered.

"Hello, this is Mayor Frank Lombardi, please put Draco on the phone."

"Please hold one moment." The butler places him on hold then presses another button to call Draco's private line.

"It's the Mayor, he wishes to speak with you."

"Cut him over."

The butler transfers the call over and resumed his prior activity.

Draco was tall and thin. He had jet black hair and always wore casual suits which are of the finest quality. He is in his mid 40's and well maintained. His affluence is a testament to his success in criminal activities and escaping punishment of the law.

"Frank! How are you!!" Draco replied.

"Someone tried to kill me the other day. You read about it yet?" Frank replied angrily.

"I would think that by now, anyone in your shoes would be used to this. It comes with the job as you should expect. And no, I had not heard about it." Draco's tone was steady and business like and a tiny bit gravelly. His voice was not high pitched and not low pitched; it was in the middle and had no hint of any accent.

"Draco, this is serious. They almost had me; they could have killed me if they wanted to. I have a messenger that will be delivering a note to you. This note was directed at me, and I want you to see it and maybe you might know who is behind it. They didn't use their real name which you'll see."

"Sure thing Frank, you know we take care of each other. It's not easy finding a mayor as good as you."

"Draco…. Look, I need your help, and I want to know who is behind this."

"Of course Frank, don't worry. Maybe the question we should ask is, who did you piss off lately?"

"Ha ha really funny Draco."

"I'll keep in touch. We will find who this is and teach them what happens to those who disrespect authority."

Draco hangs up the phone and pours himself a glass of red wine. He presses a red button on his desk and within a few minutes Bruno walks in. Bruno was very muscular and wore a suit always. Under his suit he had two guns hidden away but readily accessible and two large knives. Sometimes he would leave the knives behind, but the guns were always with him.

"Hello Boss." Bruno said, stoic and stern.

"Hello Bruno, it seems we may have a vigilante harassing our favorite mayor. See if you can find out who it is. Work with the Blanco brothers."

"Will do Don."

***

A couple of days later officers bring in a suspect to be interrogated in connection with the Town Hall attack. Bobby was a thin young adult, 22 years old with thick curly brown hair and wide brown eyes. He is on the taller side standing at six foot even. The officer walked him into the interrogation room and sat him at one end of the table, while the interrogation officer sat at the other.

"Hello son." The officer said to the suspect.

"Hello sir."

"You know why we're here?"

"Yes sir, the other officers said you wanted to ask me questions about the town hall incident."

"That's right."

The officer looked over the report, the only sound in the room at that moment was of paper flipping over to the next page.

"Your name is Bobby, right?"

"Yes sir." Bobby saw that this officer was a tall figure which he estimated at about 6'2", slightly taller than him, with a thick build composed of muscle under fat. He had a military haircut and a pale complexion.

"My name is Officer Sezowich." He flipped a page then

continued "I see you were identified to us as a lookout. Is that right?"

"...." There was no response from Bobby.

"Bobby, I have been interviewing people for many years, and I want you to know that I'm on your side here. I want to get you out of this room and back home as quickly as possible." He looked over to Bobby, gave a smile then continued the questioning.

"can you tell me if you were asked to be the lookout for someone?"

"Sir, I decline to answer." Bobby said shaking and pale white.

"I understand your reluctance. But I can promise you this will not go well for you if you don't cooperate."

"Sir, I respectfully decline to answer." Bobby continued.

"Bobby, I want you to know that you are not in any trouble...YET. The best thing you can do is help me, then I can in turn help you."

"..." Bobby made no response again.

"I will be right back Bobby." He said as he stepped out of the interrogation room. He made his way into another office.

"Well, how does it look?" Mark asked.

"He is not talking."

"Keep on him, we have enough linking him to the crime we just need him to make a mistake."

"Have you spoken with Detective Warn regarding this?" Officer Sezowich asked.

"Don't worry about him. We are both working on this case. I will update him on it later. I would like to be able to tell him we have our guy so stay on him."

He went back into the interrogation room and continued the questioning.

"You should know that everyone in that town hall was targeted with a gas attack. You are very lucky no one was seriously injured or you could be charged as an accomplice to attempted murder."

He looked over to Bobby, through his dark glasses he read the body language. Bobby was clearly terrified, and he could see his tactics were working. He loved interrogating with dark glasses because no one could tell what his eyes were doing, and he was always looking at specific body parts when reading suspects. He paid attention to hand placement before, during, and after certain questions, leg positions, breathing, he was an expert. He pressed on some more.

"Bobby, do you know anyone personally with the skills to climb the way this person did within the building?"

"Sir I respectfully decline to answer." Bobby stated.

"Bobby, I think you don't understand the seriousness of this situation. I have interviewed many people both guilty and innocent. I can tell you if you don't start cooperating things could go badly for you. You could face criminal charges and 30 years in jail."

He looked over to Bobby and saw him trembling.

"Now, do you personally know anyone with archery skills?"

"I decline to answer."

The questioning continued for another 6 hours. Bobby was now very tired and concerned he was in deep trouble.

"Look Bobby, I want us both to be done with this. Let's try again." The officer was getting tired as well but hid it perfectly.

"Remember Bobby, I'm on your side here. Now tell me, what were you doing outside the town hall that evening. I already know the answer to this so you should not be afraid to answer at least this question."

"I was standing lookout." Bobby replied and the officer was now elated but still kept his emotions from Bobby. He lied to Bobby about knowing why he was there, but the trick worked and he got his victory on two fronts, the answer to the question and the answering of the question.

"That's great Bobby, we are making progress. Now about my other question, do you know anyone with archery experience?"

"No sir."

Excellent! The officer thought. He has broken. The questioning only lasted another hour before Bobby unknowingly confessed to being an accomplice and partner in crime. Unfortunately for Bobby he was in serious trouble. Later that afternoon Patrick was informed by Officer Sezowich that Bobby had confessed.

"Is that right Officer?"

"Yes, I was going to deliver this message to Mr. Pull but since I ran into you first and I know you were anxious to get the confession I figured I'd deliver the news directly."

"I was anxious for a confession?" Patrick asked, puzzled.

"Yes, that's what Mr. Pull told me unless I miss heard him."

"Thank you for the updates Mr. Sezowich."

They parted ways and Patrick made his way back to his desk. It was very disconcerting what he was told, but then again, the officer could not be sure if he heard correctly. More disturbing was the fact that it seemed like a confession may have been coerced. It is an ugly practice that happens more than it should, he thought. Looking out the corner of his vision he saw Mark walking in the hall and went out to meet him.

"Mark, the case is closed regarding the town hall situation." Patrick said angrily.

"Really?"

"Yes, they have a confession from an accomplice and believe he may have been behind the whole thing."

"Oh interesting. That was fast."

"Yea I thought the same."

"I guess we can focus on our other cases."

"It would seem so but I'm still going to poke around on this one. I like getting answers as you know and for this case all I have are questions."

"Yea, I can understand it. This city is going to shit." Mark hid his frustration from Patrick.

"Would you be able to give me a ride home today?" Mark asked, changing the subject.

"Sure."

The car was mostly silent as Patrick drove. He broke the silence with a question he posed to Mark.

"By the way, Officer Sezowich said you told him I was eager for a confession?"

Mark looked over at Patrick who never broke his stare away from the road.

"I think he misunderstood. What I told him was that we were eager to catch the assailant and we should press all suspects hard."

"I see." He replied stone faced.

"You can drop me off here." Mark got out of Patrick's car and waved goodbye.

The car resumes its course, and Patrick is lost in thought. "Something's not right" he thinks to himself. As his drive comes to an end he pulls into his driveway, gets out of the car, walks inside his home and kisses his wife Martha. At dinner Patrick played with his fork instead of eating.

"Where is Kevin?" Asked Patrick.

"He is at his friend's house." Martha replied.

"Oh right, tonight's movie night." He played with his fork some more.

"What's bothering you honey?"

"This case I'm working on was suddenly resolved. Some kid confessed to it."

"That's good, isn't it?"

"They supposedly have their assassin. That's what I was told when I was asked to close the case."

"Oh, that happens sometimes, doesn't it?

"Confessions happen yes but unfortunately they are sometimes, perhaps most times, coerced."

"Oh!"

"Don't worry babe. I will investigate it and find out what's going on. There are so many crimes with dead leads in this city maybe I'll get lucky with this one."

Patrick planted the fork into his spaghetti and began twirling it then started eating while staring into the distance.

"You have a great reputation at the precinct." She said as she ate.

Patrick's stare remained unbroken.

***

Carinne has been scanning the newspapers every day since the incident at the town hall meeting hoping that her actions would have caused enough of a ripple in the sea of corruption engulfing the city to bring this incident into the spotlight, but very little had been reported. Her note to Frank was never mentioned.

"He must have destroyed it." She thought.

She stroked one hand down her long blonde hair. She had a very athletic build that she worked on daily. Her chest, abs, and arms were toned but her legs were large and well-muscled. If she needed to physically engage an opponent, it would be mostly kicks to subdue them. Her arms were dedicated to climbing and hurling projectiles. She stared at the newspaper looking for more reporting. An intense focused look beamed though her big blue eyes. She continued scanning the paper then came across an article claiming that one of the assassins had been apprehended and confessed to the crime.

"What! How!!" She whispered out loud.

The article went on to say that the name of the assassin is Bobby Gray. He was arrested two days ago then immediately convicted due to the confession.

"Damn it!" she thought to herself. "I told him to keep quiet. I should have known better. I should not have involved him!"

She closed her eyes in frustration. She might be able to correct this, but it was another complication she did not need. Her apartment was very sparse with random exercise weights lying about and some olympic rings hanging from a pull up bar in one corner of her open studio. It was a small space but the fact that it was an open space with tall windows and high ceilings made it seem larger than it was. She began her morning routine of weightlifting followed by chin ups then pushups using olympic rings followed by pull ups and other exercises on the rings adjusting their height as needed. She worked a large muscle range in her arms and chest. The kinds used for climbing. She then moved on to lifting a heavy stone that weighed about 75 pounds to train both her grip and yet another set of muscles in her arms. On alternate days it would be all leg work, kicks, squats and stretches. All this while pondering her next moves against this city's seemingly infinite corruption. The focus of her strength training however would be legs to support various kicking styles. She would finish her routine with a jog and shower then head off to train her students in gymnastics. The exercise helped her focus her rage and for brief moments substituted one pain for another.

The following day Patrick had scheduled to meet with Bobby. He was very tired; he barely got any sleep. Bobby's situation was eating away at him, and he needed to speak with Bobby. His conscience demanded it. Bobby was seated in an interview room used for convicts. It had a barrier separating the convict from the interviewer. Patrick walked in and took his seat opposite Bobby who was in his jail fatigues.

"Hello Bobby, my name is Patrick Warn."

"Hello" Bobby replied distantly.

"I want to ask you some questions about the night of the incident at the town hall." Patrick opened up a binder and began with his first question.

"Can you tell me what exactly happened that caused you to get involved in this situation?"

Bobby looked down for a moment. He remained silent.
"Bobby, I just want to get an understanding of the situation. This is already on the record but feel free to confirm or deny anything so I can add it into what we have…For future consideration of possibly reducing your sentence."

"I was asked to be a lookout." He looked up at Patrick. His demeanor changed from disinterest to a focused stare.

"What were you asked to look out for?"

"Anyone not doing their job." His stare still focused on Patrick.

"What do you mean by that?"

"Any official or officer that was not in their assigned place. Any press member going to areas of the building they are not expected to be in and the same for the general public."

Patrick thought about this for a minute then asked.

"What were you supposed to do if anyone diverged from their expected route or role?"

"I was to point to the sky for a full minute."

"And what else?"

"That's it."

"That's it?" Patrick asked curiously.

"Yea."

"It says here you had inside knowledge of the incident? You knew the assailant attacked with arrows."

"I didn't know that." Bobby replied.

"Bobby, I am looking at your responses to the officers that interviewed you. They have in their interrogation notes that when they asked you if you had any training on the weapon used you said, and I quote *"No sir, I never had any training on any weapon whatsoever, not even bows and arrows!"* and they never once mentioned what weapon was used."

Bobby paused for a minute then:

"When they interviewed me for hours and hours, they had mentioned arrow holes a lot. That there were arrow holes in the office wall and so I…I just assumed the weapon used was a bow and arrow."

Patrick closed his eyes and rubbed his head. It was clear now that this boy had his testimony used against him and he had been fed information about the incident to get him to incriminate himself and it worked.

"Thank you, Bobby, for your time. Please hang in there." Patrick got up quickly and walked away. Heavy in thought though Patrick was, he remembered that the weapon used was in fact not a bow and arrow but some type of bow gun and bolts. So perhaps there was a possibility here to help Bobby, he thought.

***

Later that day Geoff was in the central park having lunch, in both hands he held a breaded chicken parmesan hero. The tomato sauce was chunky, the bread was toasted to perfection, hard shell outer with a soft bread inner, hot and fresh, cheese dripping out from the sides. Just enough sauce to not be too messy. The cheese was stringy and delicious. After the first bite he could not help but smile and "mmm".

"Damn this is good" he thought or did he actually say it out loud. He bit down eagerly and munched away. The show attracted the attention of one, then two, then three noisy sparrows chirping and hopping about. They were followed by a couple of pigeons. The pigeons walked in circular patterns while the sparrows chirped and hopped around noisily. With every bite they got closer, all of them, the pigeons especially. Geoff went to reach for his drink and almost grabbed a pigeon that had crept up on him.

"I'd better eat faster before I get swarmed." He thought.

He broke off a small piece of bread and tossed it a few feet away from him to get some more time and breathing room and the swarm moved out in a frenzy to attack the morsel. While those birds fought over the food two large ravens landed very close to Geoff. They moved slowly and prevented the other birds from returning. A third raven landed, and this one bore a rolled paper in its beak. It walked over to Geoff and dropped its package. The three of them then flew off. Geoff finished his sandwich and grabbed the note. It looked silly, it was composed of letters clipped out of books or magazines and mashed together to make words.

It read:

"Dear Reporter, drug deal to go down on the night of the 5th. Corner of 14th and Broadway. Stay hidden and bring appropriate recording equipment."

It was simple and to the point. There was a danger here he thought. It could be some kind of setup and maybe he needed to go to the police, but then the thought came to him, they might laugh him out of the station when he showed them the note. Then another thought, how great a story it would be if he broke it. "Caught In the Act" the headline would read. The night of the 5th is 3 days away. More than enough time to prep. He looked up and around to see where the ravens had gone or to whom they had flown to. They were clearly trained but they were not visible anywhere any longer. As he left, he began putting together plans to find a safe recording spot.

***

Geoff was setting himself up on the 3rd floor of an apartment building. He made a deal with the landlord allowing him to record from one of the hallway windows facing across the street from the location specified in the note. He was 50/50 on if the tip would lead to anything but it comes with the territory he thought. A few hours later he sat in his folding chair looking out the window waiting, waiting and waiting. Then, late into the evening a car pulls up. It parks in front of a thrift shop and after a short while two people emerge, one appears to stand guard and the other walks up to the car. Geoff points the camera and zooms in. He recognizes one of the faces as Bruno, Don Draco's thug. Without wasting a moment, he realized he needs to start recording the encounter, he presses the button to start the recording but instead he fumbled the buttons and turned on the light mounted on to the camera. The flash of light is seen by Bruno before Geoff could turn it off. This folly was also witnessed by Carinne who was perched above where Bruno was. She was in her black shadow outfit and ready.

"Fuck" she said under her breath. What the hell is it with this city, is everybody just stupid or evil!

She sees Bruno and one other charge towards the building the light came from. She begins running across the roof top, climbs down a few floors using the fire escape and then hops on to a wire to cross to the other building. Meanwhile Geoff is packing his camera but then decides he should just get out while he can and begins running towards the stairs. He sees Bruno charging up towards him and as he looks up he makes eye contact with Geoff.

"Gotcha!" He yelled up to Geoff.

Bruno instructs his thug to watch the lobby and Bruno resumes running up the stairs. Geoff heads back to the window, forces it open but it's a straight fall. Can I survive a fall from this height he thought to himself then quickly turned back around only to see Bruno behind him at the other end of the hall.

Suddenly glass is heard breaking behind Bruno. The sound came from a window in the stairway. A figure dressed in black glides through the opening and starts charging towards Bruno. Bruno begins to turn at the sound of the glass breaking. Geoff sees this but is frozen in place. Carinne does a running jump kick catching Bruno off guard.

"Run you idiot" she yells to Geoff.

Geoff hears the feminine voice then remembers his peril and begins towards the elevator which is now his only way.

"Go up!" Carinne calls out.

Geoff looks at her puzzled but enters an elevator and presses the up button.

She drops a couple of cylinders that begin smoking. As they smoke, she put's distance between her and Bruno by jump stepping backward while facing him, he begins reaching for his gun. Carinne seeing the motion then throws a small grenade at him. It explodes with a mix of pepper and other chemicals temporarily blinding him. The smoke in the halls now also darkens the entire hallway. She drops to the floor and using both legs trips Bruno while he is rubbing his eyes. He falls to the ground, hard, his gun goes sliding into the darkness. In the next instant a large dagger penetrates his chest, once on the left and again on the right. He has no time to scream. Then Carinne disappears through the smoke and makes her way to the lobby. She drops a smoke bomb down the staircase which explodes on contact with the floor filling the lobby with smoke. The thug hears the sound looks over and sees the smoke cloud.

"Hey Bruno, you there?"

In the next instant the smoke parts seemingly in slow motion and through the smoke a small round silver dart breaks through, flies across the hall and makes contact with the thug's forehead. He recoils from the shock, drops his gun and places both hands on his head and collapses dead to the ground. In two heartbeats, Carinne parts through the smoke, follows up with another two stabs to the chest just to be sure. She then gets in an elevator and heads up to the top floor.

Geoff is in the hallway trying to open the emergency exit, he spins around when he hears the elevator door open, then somewhat relaxes when he sees the figure in black exit.

"Both are dead. Get your things and leave immediately!" She spoke.

"What's your name? Who are you??" He asked.

"Are you new to reporting?" She asked.

Geoff looked puzzled. "No, I've been doing this for years why do you ask that?"

"Because you're asking a masked person who they are."

"Riiiight."

She opened the window to the fire escape and sat on the sill with one leg out and one leg in and turned to Geoff.
He saw her outline clearly and she was in good shape.

"I want you to look into Bobby's case, he is innocent and if the authorities ask, say nothing about me for both of our sakes."
Then she turned and exited out the fire escape and in a blink was gone.

She is beautiful, he thought. He made out some blonde hair that started to poke out from her uniform during her scuffle. He thought her voice was lovely as well. She had saved him and taken out the thugs. He went back down to his floor and could hear people coughing and talking, the smoke was still thick. He took a deep breath, ran to the end of the hallway and grabbed his gear, sloppily and noisily, but he was still invisible in the fog. He returned back up to the broken window created by Carinne and exited with bag in hand. The police would arrive shortly after. Several of the residents had phoned the incident in to them.

Geoff did not expect any contact with the police but would be ready for it.

***

A few days later Geoff paid a visit to the 45th precinct to meet with Bobby.

"Hello Mr. Warn how are you?" Geoff asked politely.

"I am fine thanks. I understand you want to interview Bobby?"

"Yes, I am curious about his story."

"Does this have any connection to the incident I saw regarding the apartment building you were at?"

"No, I had already told the cops that I was given false information about a possible drug deal going down and had left before anything happened." Geoff said as frankly as he could sell it.

Patrick was annoyed partially as it seems luck is always on the side of crime but the fact that this reporter is concerned about Bobby was a good sign he thought.

"Follow me then." Patrick walked Geoff down the hall to an area where he could speak with Bobby then walked him over to a desk with a partition. Geoff seated himself and after a few minutes Bobby arrived and sat down opposite him.

"Hello Bobby, my name is Geoff, I am a reporter for the local paper."

"Hello sir."

"I would like to know about your accomplice at the scene. Can you tell me anything about this person?"

"I did not have an accomplice."

"The police report I have said otherwise. Maybe let's start at the beginning. I will put this aside and you tell me everything you feel comfortable discussing."

"I don't want to talk about this anymore sir."

"I understand but I would like to help you. Your situation seems strange to me and in reviewing the information I was given it seems like your own testimony was used to convict you."

"Yes, that's what happened. I was told after many hours of questions that I was hurting myself by not cooperating."

"I am pressing record now, please tell me everything from the beginning."

"I was approached by someone the night before asking for my help. They wanted me to stand watch outside of the town hall meeting and signal them by raising my hand if any officer or staff deviated from their job. Or even if any pedestrians walked to areas of the building they are not supposed to be."

"Just raising your hand?"

"If they walked away from the reception area to the sides or out of my view or acted in any way suspicious I was to point to the sky for about a minute sir."

"Can you identify the person you met with?"

"Tall, brown short hair, wearing sunglasses. The hair looked odd like it might be a wig. They did not give me their name. They paid me 100$ on the spot as we agreed."

"Male or female?"

"Male"

"What else did they tell you?"

"Nothing sir, they were translating."

"Translating? What do you mean??"

"They were being instructed by someone else. I could not see the other person."

"I don't understand…"

"It looked like sign language, with someone else out of my view. He told me to keep my eyes on him when I started looking around."

"Oh!" Geoff said in surprise, then continued the questioning.

"What else?"

"I was told not to speak to the police, not a word."

"Interesting, why didn't you follow those instructions?"

"I did for many hours sir."

"Right, I see what happened here."

Geoff looked up at the ceiling and thought to himself that they framed this boy and they had nothing at all. He knew they were not interested in looking into it further.

"Listen Bobby, I'm going to try to help you out but it's going to take some time. Hang in there." Geoff got up and started to walk away and just barely heard:

"Thank you sir!"

He nodded as he left. It was lunchtime and hunger was calling. Geoff sat down on a nearby bench and unwrapped his sandwich. He placed his bag next to him on the bench and turned his head over at the sound of fluttering. Next to him a giant raven landed on the top of the backrest of the bench. It dropped something from its mouth then flew off. Not watching the bird but captivated by the dropped object Geoff picked it up. A rolled note which when untied had a message written in red ink. The lettering was typed. It said:

"We met before; the first time was at the town hall. I was high up above you and you looked right at me, in my direction anyway. I thought I had been caught but then you looked away. When we met again, I saved you from those thugs."

Then beneath the note is signed:

-C. Durand Nov 10th

Hmm, the date is in the future or could be the past. He flipped the paper over and barely visible was the logo of the Hope City Cemetery.

He folded the note and placed it back in his pocket. He finished his sandwich then wrote a reminder to himself to pay a visit to the address on the note on November 10th.

***

It was late on the day November 10th, and Geoff was walking around the Hope City Cemetery not sure what he was looking for. It was a cold day, and snow had carpeted everything bright white. Then he saw another raven flying above him. "Could it be the same bird?" he wondered. He quickly moved to where it was flying in circles, the snow made crunching sounds beneath his feet. A black dot on one of the graves caught his eye. The bird landed on the tombstone of that grave and then flew off out of sight as Geoff approached. Geoff saw it was actually a black rose that had been left on the grave.

Carved into the stone was "Charles Durand"

The date of death was November 10th. He made note of the name then noticed the adjacent tombstones. Robert Durand and Claire Durand, Father and Mother. Charles was the son. He took notes and the dates of their deaths were in the following order: 1st the mother then the father and lastly the son. "Time to do some research" Geoff thought.

Way above looking down on Geoff was Claire with the raven on her shoulder. She watched as Geoff began to leave the cemetery. She was dressed all in black and stood at the top of the watchtower opposite the cemetery.

his walk slowed as he neared the entrance when he heard a mechanical voice say "Geoff" in a crackly tone.

"Yes? Who's there and how do you know my name?"

Just ahead of Geoff a figure steps out from around the gates to the cemetery. He was on the outside and not visible to Geoff until he stepped into view. He was very large, tall and wide. Not like any human Geoff has ever seen in person. Beneath a black felt duster hat with a round top and flat wide brim was a figure barely visible. His face mostly obscured by black fabric wrapping around only allowing his eyes to be seen. He wore a trench coat, and the torso portion had a thick sash that covered both shoulders and ran around the body down to his waist where it ended in a knot. His arms were tucked within and not visible. The pants were also black, not slacks of any kind but something like military fatigues except all black thick fabric. The boots were black but appeared to be painted metal feet instead of actual boots on human feet.

"Geoff" the mechanical voice came again "You will need a firearm." He spoke slowly and mechanically as if a recording of poor quality was being played back at Geoff.

"Who are you?"

"Geoff....I am here to help. We will meet again later. We need to work together."

"Why do you sound like that?"

"I damaged my vocal cords screaming in pain during operations to repair my arms and legs. I was sedated but not fully since I am allergic to anesthesia. Long story I can tell you later. We will part now and get yourself a gun Geoff."

The mysterious figure turned and started walking away from Geoff. Geoff took one last look and wondered what he was getting into.

***

The following day Geoff was in the basement of the Hope City Library. He thanked the clerk and made his way to a microfiche machine. He placed the slides into the machine; each slide was an old newspaper going back to when the Durand murders occurred. He slowly began reading through the headlines. The first read:

"Mother of two murdered in cold blood."

The news article continued:

"The body of Claire Durand was found Monday morning by police hounds after a long search throughout the city. The body was buried in a shallow grave in the city's central park in a remote area that was currently closed to the public. The authorities have contacted the family to make them aware. The victim was found with a gunshot wound to the back of the head. Additionally, bruises were found around the neck and on her arms. Police are continuing to investigate the crime. No suspects have been identified."

Geoff moved on and continued reading, then came across another story, this time involving the father. The headline read:

"Father of two dies at hospital after confrontation."

The news article continued:

"Robert Durand was rushed to the Hope City Hospital with two gunshot wounds, one to the chest and the other in the stomach. The police report states that while at dinner with his family he had an encounter with two men which spilled out onto the sidewalk. The authorities on scene reported that the father was not able to communicate with them due to the pain. His son was questioned but declined to make any comments."

"This is madness!" Geoff thought to himself. This family is being taken out one after the other. He resumed his research.

One last article contains the murder of Charles, the son. Unfortunately, much like the other articles, this one has no information in it. Geoff read it and had a strong feeling of DeJa'Vu. He looked again and was shocked, the author was none other than Geoff Bryson! He was the author who wrote it several years ago and forgot about it completely? It was bringing him back. It reminded him that life in Hope City came very cheaply. This became his belief back then and perhaps it had stuck, perhaps he has a terminal case of apathy. His heart sank. He re-read the article he had written to make sure he didn't miss any important details but when he had written it, he did not add any relevant information, nothing much about the victims, and he started to remember how it was just another day, another story, another murder, another victim. He rubbed his face, it felt warm, he wondered if it was red with shame at how lazy this reporting was. "I can barely remember this…." He thought to himself. He read it over again a third time then a fourth. "I am no reporter." He said under his breath.

After many hours the clerk passes by and tells Geoff the Library will be closing soon.

"Thank you for your help today, I am done for now." Geoff said as he handed the microfiche slides back to the clerk. Next stop is the gun shop he thought and then tomorrow he needs to go through police records.

***

The following day Geoff made his way back to the 45th precinct. He met with Detective Patrick Warn again to try to get more information.

"Is this document request in connection with Bobby?"

"No, or at least I don't think so Mr. Warn but I'm not sure what I'll find. I hope there is something that clears him. Innocent people should not be in in jail in a working criminal system" Geoff said as he took sips from his coffee.

Patrick nodded and smiled. The words brought him back to his early days. When criminals were criminals and cops were cops.

"Come back in a day or two. It will take me some time to gather these documents for you."

"Ok I will see you then. Thank you Mr. Warn." Geoff got up to leave.

He exited the building and started walking down the block. The cold made him grab his coat and close it tighter around him. He made a turn onto a quiet street and continued his walk lost in thought. As he rounded the corner and made his way on to another street, he noticed a car driving past him slowly, he glanced at it out of the corner of his eye. It seemed very similar to a car that had already driven past him a short while before. "Must be my nerves getting to me." He thought. He walked some more, this time more briskly. Then again, the same car was driving slowly past him. This time he acted like he did not notice.

After it passed, he crossed the street so he would be on the opposite side to try to throw it off, but it was a one way street so it was questionable how effective that would be. He began looking at the yards wondering if he could take a shortcut onto another street by cutting through them and eventually lose the car. He looked behind him and it was making the turn again crawling up to him. "Damn it!" he thought, I'll just keep walking past it." He kept calm and continued his speedy walk.

The car was pulling up again but as Geoff became parallel with the car it stopped this time, two exited, one from the rear and one from the passenger side.

"Excuse me sir. Over here, this way sir." The voice called out to Geoff, but he kept walking. Then a hand landed on his shoulder.

"Sir.... this way please…"

The hand forcefully escorted him to the car and lowered Geoff's head as he was made to sit in the back seat. The car resumed driving.

"We know you're a reporter. Your name is Geoff Bryson." The man in the back seat sitting next to Geoff said.

"We just have a few questions for ya." He continued.

"Who are you?" Geoff asked.

"We were friends of Bruno." The man in the passenger seat said.

"Who is Bruno?" Geoff asked trying to pass off ignorance.

"You maybe never met him I guess but you were at a scene where he was killed."

"I was?" Geoff lied hiding as much from them as possible.

"Yea, you were. The apartment building near the Corner of 14th and Broadway"

"I was there on an anonymous tip that said something would happen and nothing happened, at least while I was there." Geoff said, fully composed but concerned.

"An anonymous tip you say?"

"Yea, it was a simple note like a child put it together. It just told me to be there, and something would happen and be ready to record. We get them all the time and it's up to us if we follow up or not. Many times, it's a waste of time. Such as it seemed this time."

"So, while you were there nothing happened?"

"Nothing at all, I packed and left after a few hours. I'm sorry about your friend. I have no information, and I have not written anything on it because whatever occurred was after I left so I had no story and no information at all."

"Well since you are a reporter we would like a favor from you. You see we are kinda like a private security, so we are helping the cops figure this out. They work slow though. Here's my card, you do me and you a favor and you call me if something comes your way ok reporter, Mr. Geoff. You, your guys or your tips, you let me know and you let me know FIRST before you even think about writing anything."

Ok. Sure." Geoff nodded and accepted the card, it was Don

Draco's security service.

"We work with the cops ya know, but in this case, you don't say noth'n to them, so things move nice and fast and smooth."

"Got it."

"Pull over, we'll let him out here."

The car stopped and Geoff was pushed out of the back seat to resume his walk. The car pulled away speedily. Later that day Geoff arrived home at his apartment. He closed the door behind him, then hung up his coat and within a few minutes he heard a faint knocking. He turned, walked back to the door and the figure from the cemetery was there, larger than life. He raised his finger to his lips making a gesture indicating that Geoff should remain silent. He pulled out a device with a meter on it then then started waving it around Geoff. Low activity. He waved it around the doorway then it started to register something. He moved it towards the coat rack, and it buzzed with more energy this time, its indicator sliding almost fully to the right, something was found. The mysterious figure looked at Geoff's trench coat and within its inner lining he moved his hand then near the bottom of the coat he removed a device and showed Geoff. It was circular and small. The figure puts it in his own pocket, then leaves—his footsteps nearly silent despite his size.

"Just great!" Geoff thought to himself. "It feels like I'm being watched by the whole town." He closed the door then began working on his typewriter on today's news. His mind was elsewhere, and worry mixed in regularly which interrupted his focus. He got up to pace around every so often trying to focus. Then out of the corner of his eye he saw a folded note on the floor. It appears to have been dropped by his visitor just a short while ago unbeknownst to him. He opened it and began reading it. The letters were mechanically written to look like handwriting. It said:

"You need to be more receptive to clues and better at cleaning your tracks. You move as if you are sleepwalking through life. I will reach out to you again for a formal introduction. We are now officially working together."

There was nothing else on the note. His hands dropped to his sides. Then there was a loud tap at the window. A very short moment later another tap. Someone was throwing small pebbles at it. Geoff walked over and he could see across the way that same figure staring back at him from the window in the adjacent building. The figure made a motion with his hands back and forth. Geoff looked at him with a blank stare. This time the figure made the same gesture but with a piece of paper in his hands. He tore up the paper, opened his fingers far apart and let the pieces fall.

"Got it." Geoff thought to himself, and he ripped up the note.

I get it. I'm involved in something big here and I need to be very careful. He poured a glass of brandy to take the edge off and sat back down trying to write today's stories.

***

The following morning over at the Amichi Mansion two of Draco's men are eavesdropping. The sound coming in from the snooping device they planted on Geoff was clear.

"What do you hear Gianni?" Asked Tony

"Nothing, just people shuffling around placing orders. I'm in the mood for a bacon, egg and cheese on a roll with salt pepper ketchup now."

"I think he found the bug and ditched it Draco." Gianni said.

"Well, we will need to keep a close eye on him for a while and see what he's up to. It bothers me greatly that he was there when Bruno was killed. The coincidence is just too much to dismiss easily." Draco rubbed his chin as he spoke.

"We'll follow him around and see what he does but so far not much, he writes boring stuff for the local paper." Gianni said removing the ear plugs he was using to monitor the listening device.

Draco summoned his butler and asked to be put in contact with the mayor.

"Hello this is Frank."

"Hello Frank, Draco. Any leads on the town hall incident?"

"Hi Draco, I have some cops working the inmates in two prisons but nothing so far. What about you."

"Nothing here either. When is the next event?"

"We have an unveiling ceremony in the central park for a new bronze statue in a week."

"Be on alert Frank and add extra cops."

"This is in broad daylight. You don't think they would try anything would you?"

"I will have some of my men patrolling as well. Better not take any chances Frank." Then Draco hung up.

***

Geoff walked into the 45th precinct and asked for Mr. Warn. He was escorted to a desk in the back.

"Hello Geoff, here are documents relating to the Durand murders." Patrick said as he handed them over.

"I pulled this from our cold case files so technically even though these cases are more than 5 years old they are considered pending which means we can re-open them if any new leads are found." Patrick said.

"If I find anything or discover something that might be useful, I will let you know." Geoff placed the paperwork into his messenger bag.

"I want this family to find justice Mr. Warn." Geoff said as he left with the papers. He hailed a cab right in front of the station and was gone in short order. Geoff arrived home, made some tea, and began reviewing the paperwork on the Durand murders. After a few hours of reviewing case details, he decided to review the testimony. He came across one of the statements from an eyewitness. It said:

"We were just having dinner one minute, I was complaining to the waiter because my lasagna was cold then I heard a dish break, and I looked over at the sound and there were two guys at this table. One was leaning over, and I saw a server walk over to see what was going on. I think the guy seated at the table was the

father, he and the other two men went outside. That's when I heard gunshots and the boy at the table ran out, I felt so sorry for him, but he ran so fast no one could stop him."

Another eyewitness account read:

"3 men walked over from another table and one of them leaned over then he used the back of his hand to knock the plate off the table. This got my attention, then three of them plus the one guy at the table walked outside and after a few minutes I heard loud pops. The boy at the table, I think the guy's son went running outside."

Then yet another account read:

"I saw one guy come in and lean over this table with this family there. I thought they all knew each other but then he leaves, and two men come in after him. I think he stayed outside, the first guy, I'm not sure but these two after him were big and they made an argument at that table. I think one of them slammed the guy's head. I can't be sure, his back was to me, but a dish broke making a loud sound and when he moved, I could see the father at the table was red-faced."

Geoff grabbed his hair in frustration. The eyewitness descriptions were also different, some accounts described red hair on one, brown on another, and another account had them as blonde twins and yet another had one of them bald!

There were no cameras of any kind to capture anything that Geoff could find. The restaurant itself burned down a short while after so there was nothing to visit. He turned his attention to other files gathered on the victims. They contained much confusion and misdirects as well. It's all effectively a dead end.

***

3 days later Geoff is sitting at his kitchen table going through a stack of mail. He catches a glimpse of a peculiar envelope that is all black mixed in the pile. He fished it out and opened it. The note inside instructs him to go to a certain address tomorrow evening. He makes a note of the address and completely shreds the envelope.

The next evening Geoff arrives at the address as he was instructed. He goes into the lobby of the building and rides the elevator to the penthouse. The elevator doors open and Geoff steps out into the foyer. Papers, carpeting and a poster, partially readable, says "Fund raiser for" and the rest is ripped off. Different materials are lying around and random decorations strewn about.

"Over here Geoff." A feminine voice calls out.

Geoff turned and walked through the open door of a double doorway which led him into a large banquet hall. He sees a beautiful girl dressed in a jumpsuit at the other end.

"You know my name but what is yours?" Geoff called.

"I am Carinne." She held out her hand, palm down. Geoff gently grabbed her hand, he began to raise it to his lips but stopped and awkwardly shook it instead not sure which was the right move, to kiss or to shake, he went for the shake.

"Carinne, it's a pleasure to meet you."

"We've already met."

Geoff paused for a minute. His eyes widened slightly.

"Were you at the apartment building? The masked person?"

"Yes."

"You're the one that gave me the drug tip! It's a pleasure to finally meet you face to face." He remembered now and chiseled a smile onto his visage.

"Oui, c'est un plaisir de vous rencontrer en personne." Carinne responded with a big shy smile.
"You speak French." Geoff observed

"Oui, Shall we sit and talk for a bit?"

Both Geoff and Carinne grabbed a seat.

"My full name is Carinne Durand." She saw Geoff's eyes widen again.

"You may know by now that my family was murdered by the mob, specifically on Draco's orders." She continued.

"I saw the case notes, legal documents, testimony, police notes, as much as I could find but I did not read any mention of a daughter." Geoff said as he relaxed some more.

"My information was removed, cleaned out to protect me. Please be careful Geoff, you don't know what we are up against."

"I understand. I'm being careful."

"My father was going to expose him. He was killed before he could. My father got caught up in it when my mother was murdered. She accidentally witnessed something she should not have."

"I see."

"I don't know what it was, but my father went crazy researching everything he could, and he found a lot of dirt on Draco."

"I only know stories of him and some of his men. I have found almost nothing on him myself. Your father was a brave and smart man to be able to do that."

"My brother found some of the information and he was going to finish what my father started. He told me about the files and what he found. One night on his way home from doing more research we were going to meet and have dinner. I was just outside the library, and I saw him…."

Carinne started to tear up. Geoff quickly grabbed a napkin and handed it to her.

"I saw him get killed. He was shot, they tried to grab his paperwork but he held tight. The gunman ran when a crowd rushed out of the library. He was still alive and dying. He held my hand and asked me to promise him something, but he couldn't finish."

"I..I'm so sorry Carinne." Geoff leaned in to hug her and she hugged him back.

"Thank you, Geoff. I am going to avenge him and bring Draco down."

"Who are you working with?"

"His name is Willhaven. You met him already."

"Yes, the man with the mechanical voice."

"Yes, he saved me from Draco's thugs that same night. They were planning to kill me. He told me later he had been watching over me. We are…" She paused.

"We are ghosts Geoff. We were rescued into a program called VARS which stands for Victim Assistance and Relocation Society."

"I guess that would mean I was rescued before something could happen to me as well?"

"Yes, they would save people who were in danger of becoming a victim and people who were trying to expose crimes like my father and brother. They were not fast enough for them but they…saved me."

"But you're…" Geoff paused for a minute.

"You're actively attacking them you're not sheltering?" Geoff finished.

Carinne placed her hand on Geoff's shoulder and leaned in as if to kiss.

Geoff positioned his head expecting it. Instead, she whispered:

"Willhaven is not the same, he trained me, be careful, he sees all and hears all." Then she gave Geoff a long kiss on the neck. She began to pull away and before Geoff could speak, she began to kiss him on the lips. He did not resist.

Out in the distance Willhaven was staring at them

out of view, then he decided to step forth and make his presence known. Geoff and Carinne stopped what they were doing at the sound of footsteps approaching. They were heavy and loud on the wood floor.

"I have trained Carinne in self-defense and I will train you as well."

Geoff was silent and focused.

Willhaven used one arm to begin untying his sash slowly. 4 arms begin to spread as the sash falls, two are robotic fully and two are partially robotic from the elbow to the hands. Geoff's jaw dropped, Carinne stared with sadness in her eyes then she looked down to the floor.

"It is a pleasure to finally meet you Geoff. Do take note that I have rescued you."

"I was not in any danger yet, was I?"

"That's because of me." Willhaven said too matter of factually.

"The listening device!"

"Geoff, when I saved Carinne I was only human. Nothing mechanical or otherwise."

Willhaven looked over at Carinne.

"Carinne, you already know this story, I would like you to keep watch. This will be brief, I promise."

Carinne made her way to cover the elevators but stood at the entryway keeping an eye on Geoff as well.

"Geoff, Carinne pulled you into this without my approval, reckless, dangerous even, but here we are."

Geoff looked very closely at Willhaven. There was a secondary sash.

Willhaven then began removing the second sash which only covered the rib cage. It fell off revealing that the top of his chest was some type of metal.

"Go ahead, touch it."

Geoff pressed a finger against it.

"What type of metal is this?"
"It's a new kind of polymer actually, it's a composite of many materials, metal included."

"This is incredible!" Geoff was looking over Willhaven with both fear and curiosity.

"I was saved twice as part of VARS. A program started by a very rich man when he contracted a life-threatening disease. The program was his way of… redeeming himself he thought. In the early part of the program, some with exceptional skill and determination would assist in salvations. I was one. But I got caught by Draco. He tortured me in a manner that cost me dearly. The mechanical enhancements you see now are where there should be human limbs."

"This is terrible Willhaven. Horrific."

"I did not die, however; my will was as steel. I was transported somewhere secret and top scientists paid by the program reconstructed me into this."

Geoff was silent.

"I am allergic to anesthesia Geoff." Willhaven stated and paused for a long minute.

Geoff looked at him uncomfortably and was about to speak to break the silence but then Willhaven continued:

"Geoff if you want, you are a reporter after all, reach out to Steve Kline. He is the neurologist that created my mechanical body. It's very hard for me to discuss this. I have fully taken over this program now, much to his chagrin. We need to work together. You will return here in the evenings after the statue unveiling."

"I have to report on that unveiling so..." Willhaven cut him off.

"You will not report on it." He said ominously

"Willhaven, I have to it's my j..." Willhaven cut him off again.

"No, you were saved once already and covering that would put you in jeopardy again, that is an event that you best avoid. You work for me now. Call out sick, quit or get fired, I don't care but you are absolutely not to be there."

"You can't tell me what to do." He slammed his fist on the table.

"You think I can't but for your sake, and especially Carinne's you'd better listen."

Geoff looked at him puzzled, "was that a threat?" He wondered.

"See you soon Geoff" Willhaven slammed one foot into the floor and with tremendous force jumped into the darkness above, a jump covering at least twenty-five feet easily, the floor shook Geoff and everything around him that wasn't nailed down.

***

Later that evening the cold night air and a full moon teamed up to witness a spectacle unfold. Willhaven is leaned against a light post, his glare fixed on Gianni Blanco who is quietly having dinner with his family across the street. The restaurant is Dino's and the atmosphere inside is warm, jovial and calm. The amber lighting giving way to candles at each of the tables further enhances the environment. Gianni raises a fork full of food; eyes fixated on his wife. Back outside a police car pulls up to

Willhaven:

"Hello Sir, everything ok tonight?" The officer asks as he leaned over and rolled down the passenger side window. Willhaven signaled back in sign language.

"Oh, you're a deaf mute?"

"Willhaven looked over, made some more signs, more forcefully."

"Ok, well I was just checking to make sure there was nothing funny going on."

Willhaven raised his gloved hand and tipped his hat to the officer. He was careful to keep his other pair of arms always hidden until needed.

"Have good night sir." Then the window rolled up and the cop pulled away.

Willhaven had a very small pebble in his other hand. He tossed it up and caught it repeatedly while watching Gianni. After a few minutes he hurled it to Gianni's face upon which the window acting as a barrier prevented it from connecting with Gianni's large nose. The click on the window got their attention as multiple heads looked out but immediately the family went back to their conversation. Another small pebble clicked against the window. The entire family only looked briefly but Gianni scanned longer and eventually made out Willhaven. When they made eye contact Willhaven removed his hat and bowed to Gianni.

"What do we have here some fucking nut." Gianni thought to himself.

"Hey Donna, I need to step out for a minute. Be right back."

Gianni wiped his mouth and threw the napkin down. He grabbed his coat as he walked out of the restaurant and swiftly made his way over to Willhaven.

"HEY YOU!"

Willhaven pointed to himself.

"YEA YOU! What's your problem interrupting a man having dinner with his family?"

"What was your problem when you interrupted a man's life because your boss was bored." Crackled Willhaven.

"What the hell is wrong with your voice? Look weirdo, go home, I'm in a good mood tonight, here's ten dollars go have some fun somewhere else." Gianni pulls out a ten-dollar bill and moves to slam it into Willhaven's chest but one of his mechanical arms acts automatically and catches Gianni's wrist. The ten-dollar bill glides to the frozen ground.

"What the fuck!" Gianni yells and pulls.

Willhaven releases and Gianni stumbles backwards.

"You pick that up and disappear, I'm going back to finish my dinner." Gianni turned.

"Enjoy it because it's your last." Willhaven crackled.

"Why you mother fucker!" Gianni turned back, pulling aside his coat, he put his hand on a revolver.

"Look buddy I'm giving you one more chance." Gianni said, keeping his hand tucked.

"Tonight…you will die. Enjoy your dinner." Willhaven turns, climbs the light post, palm over palm using his two half-human arms and the balls of both mechanical feet. In two blinks he was at the top then jumped to a tree, then several more jumps and all Gianni could see at this point were tree branches shaking from Willhaven's movements. The branches trembled going further and further into the distance until he could see no more activity. He turned, ran back inside and without hanging his coat demanded the bill, ordered the family to get their things, and they drove home. Willhaven was perched on the roof of Gianni's home and watched the car pull in with the family and thought "dumb move Gianni, very dumb." He prepared himself by pulling down the armored face from his hat. The garage door opened slowly, and they disappeared into the home. Gianni ran to the phone and began to call Draco but the phone was dead. Upstairs a window is heard being smashed through.

"Everybody back in the car." Gianni yelled but before anyone could move Willhaven was at the top of the stairs looking down on the family.

"It's you! you stupid fuck!" Gianni yelled.

"Donna, get in the car and drive to your mothers house NOW!"

Willhaven jumped down the entire flight of stairs and was in front of Gianni. A gunshot was fired and Willhaven tilted to one side just enough to dodge then came another which embedded a bullet into Willhaven's over armor on his chest, then he grabbed Gianni, lifted him with one fully mechanical arm and slammed him to the ground, the wood planks caving in and parting from the pressure. Willhaven turned to the wife and kids:

"Do not try to fight me, you won't win." He turned his attention back to Gianni's grumbling and moaning and tosses him over one shoulder like a bag of laundry.

"What are you going to do to him!" Donna yelled at Willhaven.

"I will give this back to you tomorrow, at the statue unveiling. Make sure you are in attendance. And it would be best if it's just you." The voice said popping and crackling.

Gianni began to speak but Willhaven covered his mouth. He took possession of Gianni's gun, putting it in one of his coat pockets. He turned and started walking up the stairs. Donna was staring in total shock. Willhaven's movement was fast, but his walk was robotic, one leg then the other then repeat in identical stop motion like movements. Then Willhaven jumped out the window and she could hear him jumping away with his prize. Gianni was getting dizzy seeing tree after tree after tree. He would feel Willhaven's landings and jumps. His view that of a bird peeking out from inside a tree then suddenly he would feel strong g-forces with each jump, and he would see his view zoom backwards out from the tree he was just in and new branches would pull forward from behind him until finally he was now on rooftops. On the rooftops Willhaven ran smoothly and quickly, Willhaven dropped through a hole in one roof into an empty attic and put Gianni down then removed his coat.

"You won't need this ever again." He crackled as he tossed the coat off to the side. He then removed the gag.

"What do you want, I'll do anything. Just let me call Draco. He can have any amount of money ready fast you hear me."

"You still don't understand Gianni; I am here to collect on your debt. My currency is life, something you think you can bargain with. I'm going to collect your debt now."

No further sounds are heard then the lights go out.

The following day the crowd is seated, the statue is still draped, the last speaker, Frank, is making his speech. Draco's men have scoured the park but find nothing of interest. The police are assembled in many small groups scouring multiple areas of the park in tandem. The cold is unyielding, and the sun offered no warmth. Donna is in the crowd and so is Draco and Tony. The main crowd is focused on Frank. Draco and Tony continuously scan all areas leaving and returning randomly after checking in with their teams. Then we hear:

"And now for the moment we have all been waiting for." Frank smiled and turned to a team of three to pull the covers off the statue. As the drapes fell, a slight breeze kicked up, sending cold air through the crowd causing everyone to grab themselves and pull their coats into their chests, the breeze bubbled up the cloth making the unveiling even smoother and more effortless. Camera flashes began going off as the drapes fell capturing every moment.

The statue was of a General on horseback, the City's founder Jebediah Hope, his horse was reared on its hind legs. On the horse's chest Gianni's corpse was tied. Jebediah was seated with a saber pointed forward and on the saber's tip Gianni's severed head was impaled. Donna let out a scream that evacuated birds from every tree. Draco could be heard demanding them to stop photographing and Frank was working to try to get the cover back on. Officers began to fill the scene causing greater chaos and confusion. Willhaven was in a nearby bell tower overlooking the scene, the sun's direction having been behind him, caused his form to be fully shadowed.

***

Much later that same day Geoff was tossed down to a large, padded mat during his training session. A hand comes into view offering to help him back on his feet, it belonged to a cloaked figure in martial arts fatigues. Carinne, also masked, was sitting off in the distance as a spectator. Willhaven stepped into view and ordered both Geoff and his opponent back to starting positions to face each other. Willhaven was nearly entirely covered as well but his face was exposed. Geoff could clearly make out his features, especially his black eyes and dark hair. Willhaven began speaking to Geoff:

"When your opponent comes in, to attack, focus on his arms and legs." Willhaven spoke more fluidly and with less static from the electronic voice box. The speech was faster and had more inflection, lively even.

Geoff nodded in acknowledgment.

"You will prepare for either leg sweeps, tosses, blocks or counters as I showed you. If you dodge a punch or other arm based attack, use the momentum of your dodge to move into your next stance. We practiced three scenarios, so he (Willhaven pointed to Geoff's opponent) is only allowed to attack you using any of those three types of attacks. There are of course many more but these three represent core motions that encompass most scenarios."

Geoff nodded again.

"Ok, let's begin the next round. At your marks. GO!" Willhaven quickly stepped out of the way after the start signal and watched closely. Geoff's opponent began stepping towards him, both arms pointed forward. Geoff took notice of his leg positions and posture. When his opponent took a swing, Geoff caught the motion of the torso as the attack wound up, and in very little time stopped his own motion, shifted his feet to dodge the punch, tilted his own torso backwards just enough, the punch swings past his jaw, Geoff felt the breeze and in the next moment Geoff caught his opponents arm and pushed it forward and twisted it to the side causing his opponent to fall forward which allowed Geoff to get his arm around his opponents neck and his leg around his opponent's leg, Geoff then tossed his opponent face first into the mat at which point Willhaven called the match for Geoff.

Geoff now lowered his hand to pull up his opponent. Willhaven addressed Geoff with a slight tone of excitement.

"That was excellent. You are beginning to develop the muscle memory and coordination that you will need. Keep up the stance practice as much as you can when I am not around. We will regroup again in a couple of days for more training. Geoff, I would like to discuss something with you privately, meet me at that desk." Willhaven walked over, grabbed a brief case off to the side which was out of view and pulled out a small book, then went over to the desk to meet Geoff. He did not sit but signed a check and handed it to him.

"Is this a paycheck?"

"Yes Geoff, you work for me now as we agreed. We are a team now and I will need a lot of your time every so often so this will support you as you step away from your old life."

"My… old… life." Geoff said out loud and thought about what he might be getting into, but he remembered there was really no choice. He looked at the check. Willhaven motioned everyone to disperse.

"Goodbye for now Geoff." Willhaven turned and left.

"Geoff…" A voice called him from behind. He turned to meet the masked figure.

"Carinne is that you."

"Yes. You did well on the mat."

"Thank you. When everyone else leaves they just disappear but when I leave it's through the front door. Is that going to change? It feels weird actually."

Carinne laughed from behind her mask then said:

"You don't have the skill yet. You're fine. I also sometimes use the door. I think I will use it today actually. Let's walk out together."

Geoff smiled and grabbed his coat and removed his mask. Carinne also removed hers and got her things. As they made their way out Geoff asked her:

"Carinne, I would like to go out to dinner with you."

"Oui, et moi aussi, yes, me too. But we need to be careful."

"I know the rules, the face paint covers the face, the mask covers the paint. We work in the darkness. We are the darkness. To show our identity is to lose our life. But it's just a date, no work involved."

"You never know when work will call."

"You mean if something happens that we are witness to?"

"Yes?"

"I think we can let our guard down for one night. I have a nice place picked out. Upscale, you will like it."

Carinne smiled at Geoff which he returned with a smile of his own. He went on to say:

"I will be quitting my reporting job Carinne, but I wanted to help Bobby first."

"We can work together to help him, but the system is broken Geoff."

They finally made their way to the lobby area and Geoff looked over to Carinne.

"Can I get your number."

She smiled and nodded. Geoff pulled out one of his pads and took her number down. As they exited the building they went in different directions but were still mentally linked. Back at the Amichi Mansion yelling could be heard.

"Draco are you fuck'n CRAZY!" Frank yelled so loudly Draco almost didn't need the phone to his ear.

"FRANK! LISTEN! What happened in the park, this is serious."

"OH, NOW IT'S SERIOUS TO YOU!"

"Frank, calm down. My security guards need clearances to carry heavy weaponry. This will have to get your approval."
"Draco, I can't do that."

"Frank, this is me taking this serious."
"Draco, if they get happy with those toys I'm finished for letting them have it."

"Frank, I will let you think about it because if they don't get them, we may both be finished." He slammed the phone onto its base.

Draco called for Tony Blanco and within a minute he was in Draco's office on the second floor of the Amichi mansion.

"Tony, we are going to find out who did this to your brother and get them. First, however, we need machine guns, grenades and rocket launchers. I need you to work with Frank on expediting the legalities in this city and at the same time work on acquiring them."

"I got it Draco."

"That's all… And don't worry, we will get them." Draco was red faced and angry and although not screaming any longer, he still spoke loudly.

Tony turned and left.

Draco turned around in his chair and poured a glass of red wine from the cabinet behind his desk and looked out the window as he took a sip. Gianni's body did not have a note on it and there was no further information from the police regarding leads of any kind. That reminded him of other sources he has not considered yet.

He turned around in his chair facing his desk again and pressed a button. After a voice answered, one of his staff, he asked them to connect him with the head of the local paper.

"Hello, Darby here who am I speaking with?"
"This is Draco Amichi."

"Hello Draco, I would like to thank you for your generous donations over the years. To what do I owe this call?"

"The incident in the park, I want all leads as you get them. I also want to speak with the reporters you had there that day."

"Sure Mr. Draco that won't be a problem. His name is Ken; he covered the story. I will ask him to pay you a visit. We don't have leads or any information at all, however. Do you still want to meet with him?"

"You have absolutely nothing?" Draco said spinning his glass round and round in his hand.

"Correct."
"Yes, I will still meet with him. Thank you." Draco hung up and took another sip. He pulled out copies of notes Frank provided him regarding testimony given to the police. He combined this with notes taken from Gianni's wife regarding his abduction the night before. The only thing Draco had was a ludicrous description. The kidnapper was described as a tall, large bodied man dressed all in black head to toe. His voice was mechanical,

and it was unclear if he had actual mechanical arms or not as when they were questioned about the same features multiple times the descriptions changed slightly. Then there was the fact that Gianni was carried away like a small child. The broken window and the damage to the interior of the Blanco home lent credibility to some of the depictions of the abductor. Investigators examined some of the trees and found strange damage to the branches. This confirms that the assailant escaped through the trees. Draco envisioned a gorilla in place of any actual human man then tossed the papers aside.

"Ludicrous" he thought.

One thing he knew for sure is how unreliable people are when under stress. He has always taken advantage of that, but now it's working against him. A few hours later Ken arrives and greets Draco. He sits across Draco's desk. Draco offers him a glass of red wine which he initially declines, then Draco says:

"Ken, I want you to relax. You are my guest here and we are both professionals. Please. I have the finest wines." Draco pulled out 3 of his favorite bottles and presented each.

"Well Mr. Draco, sure why not. I will try this one." Ken pointed to the bottle in the center.

"Well Mr. Oberman, that is a fine selection. One of my best and actually my favorite." He poured a glass and handed it to Ken.

Then he poured himself a glass of the same. He smelled it then swirled it around then said:

"Cheers Mr. Oberman." Raising his glass, Ken followed the motions. Draco smiled and both men took a sip. Excellent Draco thought.

"So, Mr. Oberman, I asked you here because of the incident in the park. The body that was mutilated so cruelly was the brother of an associate and close friend of mine."

"I am very sorry to hear that Draco. My condolences."

"Thank you, Mr. Oberman. I need to know any information whatsoever you may have. I will be aiding the police investigations both financially as well as with my own legal teams where needed. Please, tell me anything and everything relating to this."

"Sure Mr. Draco, there's not much information as this event seemed to be very straight forward, just a statue unveiling after some speeches. The only oddity in the whole matter I would say is that I got a call telling me where to sit and to make sure I was in that seat for the best viewing angle. I was told I could capture facial expressions upon reveal and have a great forward view of the statue for photographs. The seating choice I was recommended was actually better than what I had chosen when I got there so I shifted over and claimed that spot, but I have never received such a mundane tip before, almost negligible."

"That's very interesting Mr. Oberman. Did the caller identify themselves?"

"No. But the voice was filled with static and crackled as if it was a recording I was listening to."

Draco paused as he made a connection with this vocal description and what Gianni's wife described.

"I assume there are no other details?"

"That's the extent of it."

"Thank you, Mr. Oberman." They shook hands and Draco turned to look out his window as he sipped his wine.

***

As Geoff slowly entered his apartment the feeling of disconnectedness continued settling in. He had just arrived home after having quit his job at the paper. There was no need to keep it any longer as Willhaven's salary would replace it and his new responsibilities would conflict with it anyway. Although his new situation is Willhaven's design it seemed to him as if there was something in the stars putting him on a new course. He sat down at his kitchen table and unrolled today's newspaper, a memento from his now previous job. Right on the front page was a blurred image of a body tied to the city's newest statue. Geoff began reading the article and was wondering what happened. Did the thug try to fight Willhaven? Was it Willhaven? He was definitely involved somehow as he had asked Geoff to avoid the unveiling entirely. Good thing he thought. The noise it's creating at his old office would just serve as an unneeded and dangerous distraction. Probably mayhem everywhere on all sides. It was extreme he thought but also, he was distant. He remembered the walk home from work over the years and how one time he tripped over a crack while crossing the street, a crack that was not there prior but is still there even today. He remembered the empty store fronts he would pass as well, now mostly boarded windows with no sign of any new tenancy in sight and the structure slowly decomposing. Willhaven had warned him to focus less and less on the news, his old life is now dead, and he needs to put all energy into his new vocation. When you do something for years it's hard to let go, it's hard to stop. Very hard. He rolled the paper up and made the motion to toss it into the garbage can but then just tossed it back on the table instead. Tonight, he had his date with Carinne and wanted to be mentally ready. He put on his workout clothes and began practicing stances and moves Willhaven had taught him as a distraction. He did this for a few hours.

***

The cold brisk air was seeping in from a slit in the window Geoff opened earlier that afternoon to air out his place and cool him down during his training. It reminded him to get ready. It was his first date in some time and he felt on edge even though he had become comfortable around Carinne. There was a lull in his social life which he thought might be making him more tense than he needed to be. He put on his best clothes, got himself ready and started heading out to the restaurant.

Carinne was getting ready as well and was quite tense and nervous. Much like Geoff or perhaps much worse than Geoff she had lost connection with the world of the living. She looked in the mirror and practiced happy, sad and laughing faces. Then threw some cold water on her face and shook her head smiling at how silly she was acting. She put on her makeup, then her dress, grabbed her purse and made her way to meet Geoff.

The Restaurant was called Aegean Coast, and it had fine Mediterranean food and drink. It provided very upscale dining in Hope City, something that is hard to find these days. The locale sat on a nicely lit street adorned with high end shops. The block was very clean, meticulously maintained in fact. The street was not asphalt but cobblestone which preserved the city's earlier days and splendor. Perched on a rooftop across the street Willhaven was using compact binoculars to view Geoff and Carinne with a watchful eye. He was perfectly camouflaged in the evening night. His spot was just below a large tree branch that overhung the rooftop. He adjusted his binoculars to zoom into their faces then using his own vision he zoomed in further. He was reading their lips as they spoke.

"Carinne, I quit my job today. Handed in the letter formally then met with my manager one last time on my way out."

"That's good news Geoff; we will be able to work together more often."

"Yes, I was also thinking about you, when I did it. I want to help you, and I want to clean up this town."

"Geoff, I can handle myself. You don't need to fuss. I also want to clean up this town, it's hard, it feels like no matter what I do things just get worse. I like to think maybe at least I'm slowing it down, but it does not feel that way." She took a sip of her drink.

"I have to bring up something a bit uncomfortable."

Carinne looked over to Geoff with interest.

"It's ok Geoff. What's on your mind?"

"I looked at today's news, didn't read the whole story but one of Draco's thugs was mutilated and put on display during the statue unveiling."

"Yes, I know."

"You do? Was it…"

"Yes, it was Willhaven."

"Did that bother you? The extremeness of it?"

"We are dealing with the most evil people imaginable. I don't feel anything anymore except hate. Until I met you Geoff."

Geoff smiled at Carinne and grabbed her hands and held them on the table.

"Carinne, I don't shed tears for them, but I did not sign up to…"

"I know… I have never done anything like that or even close to it. I have thought about it and Willhaven has stopped me from interacting with them directly every time."

"He has?"

"Yes, he says death is his domain."

The waiter arrived with their food.

"Sorry to interrupt your moment, your meals are here."

"Thank you." Carinne responded and smiled.

As they ate the topic changed to things that were beginning to bore Willhaven. After some time, he decided the conversation shift was of no further business or importance. The evening did provide Willhaven with much needed information. He felt now more than ever he would be able to help Carinne. Both her and Geoff actually. The binoculars were lowered and pocketed. He began looking around the area directly below him. He saw bums in more numbers than he should, he saw suspicious individuals walking about, no police anywhere either on foot or by car. He could hear sirens very distantly. It was a sharp contrast to where Carinne and Geoff were enjoying the evening. He then silently vanished into the darkness. The following day Geoff decided to look into Willhaven's story further. He had a lot of questions which Willhaven was not open to speaking of, but he did offer up someone who could speak to it for him. "Let's see, Willhaven mentioned Stephen Kline" Geoff thought to himself as he was leafing through a stack of information at the library. Old newspaper articles Geoff had reviewed one after another lay in a pile on one side of the desk. He would then cross reference information eventually narrowing down the various Stephen Klein's to smaller and smaller results until he found a perfect match. A Hope City University graduate who went on to patent numerous medical devices for aiding people who suffered brain damage or other neurological disorders. "Fascinating" He thought. He made note of the phone numbers then headed home.

Back at his apartment he sat down and pulled out the number and called.

"Hello this is Stephen."

"Hello Stephen, my name is Geoff Bryson. I am calling you to discuss a matter regarding Willhaven."

The line was silent.

"Hello? Stephen are you still there?"

"Yes, I'm sorry. I have not heard that name in a few years. What is it you would like to know?"

"Anything you can tell me. He was not comfortable discussing the circumstances regarding his… abilities… I'm not quite sure yet what I would ask you, but he mentioned you as saving him and I would like to understand him better."

"I see. Well maybe it's best if we have this conversation in person. I will give you my address and you can stop by tonight if it's urgent enough."

Geoff took the address then resumed the conversation.

"Thank you Stephen. I would say it's very important, not quite urgent, but the sooner I understand him the easier certain things will be I think."

"See you shortly."

***

Geoff scooped up his notebooks, pens and coat, then flew out the door and began heading over to the Klein residence. Geoff's car pulled up into the large driveway alongside a BMW 1800 in new condition. The house was a Tudor style home, on the edge of the city, a quaint and quiet neighborhood. Many rooms were lit and gave a welcoming glow out into the yard. Geoff jogged up the walkway which was lit by lamp posts and rang the doorbell.

"Hello, Geoff I presume?" Stephen put his hand out to greet him.

"Pleased to meet you Stephen."

They entered the warmth of the home leaving the night behind. They both sat in the living room in front of the fireplace which was lit and crackling.
"Would you like anything to drink Geoff?"

"I'm fine."

"If you don't mind, I'm going to have a glass of whiskey."

"Sure, go ahead."

"So, you want to know about Willhaven?" Stephen asked as he poured himself a shot, its amber glow lit by the ambiance from the fireplace. He swirled the glass under his nose taking in the scent.

"Yes, I work for him now and his physical and mental state

seem… seems extreme to me."

"I see. Are you a rescue Geoff?"

"Willhaven would say so."
"What do you say?"

"I suppose I am. He saved me from a possible negative situation. I had a bug planted on me which if left unnoticed I think would have gotten me and another and possibly even Willhaven himself in some kind of trouble with the mob."

"Then I would agree with Willhaven on it. So, I assume this means you are aware of the VARS program?"

"Somewhat yes."

"The program was created by Terrence Leighwind III in his final years. He wanted to use his massive wealth to help bring criminals to justice and protect those who were victimized."

"I see." Geoff was taking notes feverishly.

"The program had reached a very advanced technological state when Willhaven joined. I was the lead neurologist, and I had contributed many lifesaving measures for victims that suffered nerve damage and severe head trauma."

"You don't work for the program anymore?"

"I am afraid not. Willhaven has taken over the entire program. He controls the funds and therefore the staffing. He closed down elements of the program he deemed to be crossing a line that should not be crossed. My part of the program was crossing one such line."

"Do you know what he meant?"

"Geoff, there was an incident that occurred prior to the changes in Willhaven's attitude. He was not like this at the start. He was going to rescue Carinne and bring her into the VARS program for protection. She had been targeted by the Mob, Draco specifically, to close the loop on that family, the Durand's. He felt there would be no more threats from them exposing anything and he was not certain what exactly she witnessed the night of her brother's murder. Willhaven had been tracking her and was one step ahead of them but when they arrived at Carinne's home Willhaven was hiding in the tree looking down."

Stephen took another sip then another and continued:

"Willhaven took two of them out with well placed daggers but the third gunman did not die from his wound and he was very mobile. Willhaven dropped to finish him off but there were others pulling up behind him, he was quickly overpowered then carted away. This was what was reported by those that were with Willhaven that terrible night"

Geoff noticed the tone had shifted in Stephen's voice, it was shaky.

"Please take it slow if you need to. I know it's tough recalling this."

"Thank you Geoff, I'm ok." He took another sip.

"As I was saying, Willhaven was captured. They tortured him then left him for dead. He was not working alone, he had scouts, other shadows, who found the location of where his body was dumped. They brought him directly to our facility. Our medics and I worked to stabilize him."

He poured a second glass and paused for a moment then continued:

"Geoff, we could not use anesthesia due to his alergy. As we worked, he screamed the entire time. The medics could change shift, but I could not. I played classical music at high volumes to drown out his screams. That was a mistake on my part."

"Oh my GOD!" Exclaimed Geoff.

"His screams stopped after some time, I don't know when exactly, but I noticed at one point that I could not hear him at all and lowered the music until it was completely mute. I looked over at him and could see his mouth motioning as if he was still screaming but only breaths came out. He completely damaged his vocal cords in this process Geoff."

"This is terrible. I can't believe this!"

"We spent the next months retro fitting him with mechanical implants which you have no doubt seen right?"

"Yes, I have."

"He is very much a weapon Geoff, make no mistake about how deadly he is. In addition to the implants, we added an extra set of arms, fully mechanical. We also bound an artificial intelligence in him to his mind so he could directly control these mechanical limbs. This artificial intelligence would sit in the middle of his brain and body, read his thoughts and turn them into actions for his prosthetics. It also would interface with him and provide solutions to scenarios, enhance his memory exponentially as well as giving him many incredible abilities that a normal person would need training on. Examples of this would be sign language and lip reading and understanding different languages he has never heard before. He could also read emotions from body language and facial expressions."

"I think I would like a glass as well…" Geoff was tense and hoped some alcohol would help.

"Here you go." Stephen handed him the glass then continued:

"There was a last step we needed to do. This was connecting his spine to robotic parts of his body. This would be the most painful part, but it would be brief as all the connectors would simultaneously inject into his spine."

Stephen looked at his glass, paused a few moments then looked over at Geoff.

"When I initiated the final step, I saw Willhaven's body fully convulse and then relax again. The heart monitors and life systems all flat lined. He was dead. They were unable to resuscitate him. I asked the team to leave us alone while I disconnected everything. After Willhaven was fully separated from nearly all machinery in the room his voice box began activating. The heart monitor was still connected and still showed a flat line Geoff."

"Willhaven was dead?"

"Yes Geoff, this voice box is part of his prosthetics. We added it after he damaged his own vocal cords so he could use it to communicate, of course with the AI as the intermediary in between. Well, the crackling came again with a voice. The voice said my name slowly and phonetically."

"Was he still dead?"

"Yes Geoff, I looked over again. It was still a flat line. Then the voice came again addressing me by my name and said that I had breached the boundary between life and death. I asked if I was speaking to Willhaven and the voice responded that he was dead and that I already knew this, but it would be sending him back here to do it's bidding and restore the balance of life and death in Hope City."

Geoff was surprised at the response, he took a long drink of the whiskey then asked:

"Did it say anything else?"

"No, when it finished the heart monitor registered a faint heartbeat which prompted me to reconnect some of the measuring equipment. I could see the body was coming back to life. The voice box crackled again but it was Willhaven trying to speak. I told him to rest, and we transported him to another room to finish his recovery. When I spoke to him later, he had no recollection of anything. I did notice however that his manner of speaking had changed. It could be due to him having discovered the AI in his head, the artificial intelligence now speaking to him in his mind and sending and receiving thoughts."

"Can the AI control the voice box without Willhaven knowing?"

"Absolutely not. It is not programmed to vocalize directly."

"Can I have a second glass?"

"Certainly!" Stephen poured another for Geoff then continued his story.

"Willhaven began his training after his recovery, but it seemed very little was needed. Because of the AI's involvement he would recall and learn on one try. Nevertheless, we flew in some assassins from Japan to finish off his training. When they sparred, they could not best him, one of them tried a strange move on him and I saw Willhaven close his grip on the assassin, and they spoke very briefly. He seemed as if he had seen a ghost when Willhaven released his hold. I could not tell you anything else but I can give you his information so you can speak to him directly."

"Thank you, Stephen. Is there anything more? This was all very helpful."

"No Geoff, I was done with this program shortly after this incident. I am easing into retirement at this point. I think the program is an excellent program, but I regret what I had done to Willhaven. I think that was crossing a line that we ignored in our efforts to save a life."

"Thank you, Stephen, I will be on my way. Take it easy."

"Good night Geoff."

They shook hands and Geoff headed back home with even more questions.

***

The sun was breaking into Geoff's room through slits in the blinds. His eyes were still closed but the brightness of his room was penetrating through. He rubbed his eyes and looked around. He reached for the clock as he let out a yawn. It was almost 10 am and he still did not want to rise but the sun had other plans for him. Unable to sleep further he stumbled into the kitchen and began cooking bacon and eggs along with some Coffee. As he ate his breakfast, he thought maybe he might skip his training today, he was still tired, the alcohol he had when speaking with Stephen was not excessive but still ate away at his energy and will. "Nah, I can do a mild workout" he thought to himself. Nothing overly straining. He thought he would start with the movements Willhaven taught him. The movements were slow, and he practiced them over and over. He practiced his kicks hundreds of times until he could smoothly perform the motions. He remembered he would be due for more training soon.

Later that evening Geoff kept staring at the clock, a stack of papers comprised of his note taking and other reference material was lying in piles on his table. It was only 7 PM but he felt ready for bed having fallen asleep briefly a couple of times already. He grabbed the number Stephen provided him with and proceeded to call the contact.

The phone took a few seconds before it started ringing then came the voice on the other side.

"Moshi moshi."

"Hello, my name is Geoff. Do you speak English?"

"Yes, hello Geoff, how can I help you?"
The voice was youthful and feminine and her English a bit off, but Geoff could understand her.

"I would like to speak with master Takeshi."

"One minute please."

Geoff could hear them speaking Japanese in the background then a new voice comes over the phone.

"Hello Geoff, this is Takeshi."

"Pleased to meet you, I am calling to get information on someone I am working with. His name is Willhaven. I was told to speak to you regarding his training."

"Geoff, unfortunately for us both I do not know much about Willhaven."

Geoff noticed his English was very clear. Takeshi then continued:

"I was brought in to train him for the VARS program which I understand is now under his control."

"Yes, that's right it is. Can you tell me about your training with him at least?"

"Are you now with VARS yourself?"

"Yes."

"Since you are in this program now Geoff, I assume you know that I am or was an assassin?"

"Yes, I was told you were flown in to train him."

"I trained Willhaven on fighting techniques and certain deadly strikes. He learned almost instantly, and perfectly."

"So, then the training was very short?"

"It lasted only a week perhaps, but it was cut short. I cut it short due to an incident we had on a training session where I tried something and…."

There was a pause, then Geoff heard Takeshi asking for tea in the background. The conversation resumed.

"I don't know what happened, I think I got lost in the moment and wanted to kill him, he had been diverting all of my attacks, blocked everything. He did not use a sword only his multitude of arms which were nearly impossible to deal with. In a moment of irrationality, I tried to perform a death strike. He stopped my hands from touching his chest. He simply raised his hand vertically and parted my fingers and stopped the move. He then leaned into me. I tried to push him back, but his other arms grabbed me from behind and pulled me close to him. He said that the move I tried I should never use again, or it will be the last time I use it. He said he would forgive its prior uses but from this moment on I am to use it no longer then pushed me back."

"What is the move he was referring to?"

"It is a death strike, a touch of death. When it is applied on a person they will die."

"What?" Geoff could not believe what he was hearing.

"I don't know how Willhaven knew what was coming or even what it was, but he did. The voice that threatened me also did not seem like his. It came from him, but the tone was different. I never felt a fear like that in my life. I think Death spoke to me directly. I have not and will not ever use those moves again. I am retired now Geoff."

Geoff was rubbing his chin.

"Thank you, Mr. Takeshi for your candor. I have received similar warnings from Willhaven but more vague."

"Be careful Geoff, you don't know what you are dealing with. None of us do."

Geoff wanted to have another drink after that call, but he needed to begin his next round of training with Willhaven. This new knowledge did not give him any more comfort than before. It does however mark a dark alliance that might be hard to break away from. He felt both sad and fearful of Willhaven.

***

Geoff and Willhaven were facing each other in the penthouse training area. Both eyes locked in unflinching stares. After a moment Geoff and Willhaven charged at each other at the sound of a whistle, Geoff throws a roundhouse kick which Willhaven blocked with his left arm then Willhaven drops and tries to sweep Geoff but instead Geoff leaped over Willhaven's attack and landed to one side then closed distance and threw some chops with his hands which were all blocked by Willhaven. Willhaven, on his last block, turns his wrist around and catches Geoff's attacking hand and pulls Geoff closer and off to one side and tries to trip Geoff while still locked on to his hand. Willhaven then twisted Geoff's hand painfully to which Geoff performed a back flip to release tension on his wrist then a second flip to try and release Willhaven's grip. The battle continued for a few minutes more then stopped at the sound of the whistle.

"That was excellent Geoff! Beyond excellent even. I am very impressed at how your hard work has paid off."

"Good match Will!" Geoff said while catching his breath. Then he continued.

"It was thanks to you, Carinne and the team." Then he gasped for more air slowly regaining his composure. Then continued.

"But you… you held back significantly."

"I did because there is no way you can beat me in hand to hand. I only used two of my arms as all of your opponents would. Our goal here is not me training you to defeat me but everyone else Geoff."

Willhaven turned to the team and asked everyone to leave.

"We have more training Geoff."

"I can't Will, I am too tired. I am spent."

"You won't need strength for this part of your training."

Geoff walked up to Willhaven and faced him.

"Ok, what's next." He said through strained but recovering breaths.

"Simple Geoff. I am going to teach you some moves that you must practice even more rigorously than everything else. These will save your life in cases of emergency."

"Ok, I understand."

Willhaven walked up to Geoff and with a much lower tone he said:

"What I show you now you show to no one else. Doing so will result in your own death. Is this clear?"

"Yes."

"Ok, let's begin. Follow me."

Willhaven walked over to a practice dummy hanging from the ceiling. He motioned to Geoff then pointed to the dummy's chest.

"There are pressure points which you must learn to read. You will identify 3 points and apply momentary pressure to each and while you do so you will think and believe that you are declaring the action of death on the target."

Willhaven then pointed to 3 spots on the dummy's chest, closed his eyes then applied light pressure on all 3, held for a couple seconds then released."

He looked over at Geoff and asked him to repeat. Geoff placed his fingers in the same spots as he was just shown. On his left hand his pointer finger went under the dummy's right nipple area then with his right hand his pointer finger rested above the dummy's right nipple area and the thumb below it. Geoff closed his eyes, waited a moment then released.

"That's good Geoff, you have the motion down, but you did not summon Death. Do it again and exactly as I said."

Geoff furled his eyebrows and thought to himself how silly this was. Does Willhaven really think he can read minds now?? He repeated the action, he closed his eyes then he thought to himself, "now you will die" and released.

"Excellent! That's it Geoff! You will need to practice this on a living thing, unfortunately, in order to master it."

Geoff was looking over at Willhaven with a puzzled look.

"You can practice on small animals, anything will do, a rabbit, a chicken perhaps. But start practicing immediately."

Geoff nodded.

"Geoff, you don't believe me yet but remember this lesson. From now on you will be able to see the life aura of living things. You will also be able to see where exactly the right pressure points are. This should be what you identify before any battle begins, Geoff."

Willhaven then turned, grabbed his coat and walked away.

Geoff looked at his own hands believing for a moment that Willhaven was telling him the truth, but he did not see anything.

"Ok, let's play this game Will." He thought to himself then

decided to make his way to the nearest pet store.

***

Geoff sat at his table looking at the small box from the local pet store. The rustling coming from the box was made by the sound of small feet scurrying about. Geoff's tension was high, but he couldn't consciously understand why. "I can't believe I'm doing this." He thought to himself. Had Willhaven made him crazy? He opened the box slowly and looked at a small white mouse. He never liked mice or rats. He hated rats to the point that he could not stand to touch one and so opted for the mouse. He picked it up in one hand, closed his eyes and thought about death. He recalled a photograph of Carinne's brother, then her father then other crime scene photos of death he had seen throughout the course of his old career. When he opened his eyes, he saw an aura around the mouse. He blinked multiple times trying to clear it from his vision as if it were caused by watery eyes or some other temporary condition, but it remained. Geoff ran to a nearby window while still cupping the mouse in his palm and now saw the aura Willhaven spoke of around everyone walking in the street below. His glance caught a random bird perched on a wire and saw its aura as well. He went back to the table sat down and looked the mouse over. He turned it over and looked at its belly and there he saw a weak spot in the aura. Closing his eyes and thinking of death he pressed on the belly of the mouse momentarily then released. Only his pointer finger was needed. He looked the mouse over for a few seconds, but nothing seemed to be happening. The phone suddenly rang, startling him, he placed the mouse back in the box and walked over to answer.

"Hello, Geoff here."

"Hi Geoff, it's Carinne."

"Oh Hi, how are you? I was going to call you. I had my last training session with Willhaven."

"Oh, that's great news, did he give you any assignment yet?"

"No not yet. I think he needs me to master this new technique he taught me."

"What did Willhaven teach you?"

"This is going to sound crazy." Geoff stopped speaking as he walked back over to the box to pull the mouse back out and as he unfolded the top lid it revealed the mouse was dead, a small trail of blood oozing from the belly of the mouse. The belly was ripped open.

"Oh my GOD!" He yelled into the phone.

"What!? What happened? Geoff?"

"It worked! What Willhaven taught me worked!"

"What was it he taught you?"

"He taught me the touch of death…"

"The what?"

"It's weird but I can see something I was not able to see before. It's like a type of energy that surrounds everything that is alive."

"Geoff, that sounds crazy."

"Yea, I know, but it works. I need to practice it more."

"What just happened Geoff, you said it worked what do you mean?"

"I bought a small mouse to test it on. Honestly, I thought Willhaven was playing a joke, but then again I never did see any sense of humor in him so I got this mouse and tried the technique and… and it killed the mouse. Not immediately but after maybe a few seconds? A minute at most?"

"Geoff, I…I think we should meet up this weekend. I want to see this."

"You do? I need a larger animal and somewhere to practice it though."

"I have a cabin Geoff, it's where I train. It's secluded. We can go there."

"That's great Carinne. I will need to find another animal, do you think we can catch one out there?"

"I have a better Idea."
"Carinne, this is something I cannot teach anyone else because according to Will…"

"Yes? Geoff?"

There was a long pause but then Geoff recovered.

"…According to Will it would result in my death…"

"I understand. I was not going to ask you to train me."

"I wanted to get that out of the way. I would like to train you with it as a life saving measure but… I don't understand what's going on. Anyway, let's meet up this weekend. It's easier if you see it in person and your cabin will help me practice also. Thank you for the offer Carinne!"

"De rien Geoff."

"You will need to start teaching me French also."

"Oui" She laughed.

***

Carinne was driving back from the local farmers market outside Hope City, her only company was the foul smell and occasional clucks coming from the back seat. Her driving was mostly on autopilot as her mind was focused on Willhaven. She was fighting off an anger that was developing against him, the car would speed up and slow down and take curves hard as she thought about Geoff's new ability. "Did Willhaven not trust me?" she thought. She should have been taught the touch of death not Geoff, what was Willhaven planning? As the car swerved around a corner the chicken in the cage tilted in the opposite direction to counter its g-forces. The cabin came into view as Carinne pulled into the driveway. She quickly put the cage in the back yard then made her way inside. Geoff would be there soon and while she believed him, she still needed to see it with her own eyes.

About an hour or so had passed and Carinne heard Geoff's car pulling up, the gravel crackling under the tires. She went outside to greet him and gave him a hug and a kiss. They walked over to the cage and Geoff bent down.

"I can see it's aura; the pressure point is right there." Geoff pointed to the side of the chicken, the right side of its breast.

"This time I want to take count of how long it takes."

"Ok Geoff, let's go behind the cabin, a bit deeper into the woods."

"I don't think it will make a sound Carinne but that's a good idea either way."

Geoff grabbed the cage, and they started their walk. Geoff walked past targets, badly damaged attack dummies and a gymnast's area with rings. Dart holes were on every surface of every target.

"So this is where you practice?"

"Yes, watch."

They stopped walking, Carinne pulled out 3 darts from hidden pockets and threw them one after another and all 3 landed bullseye on 3 separate targets.

"Wow, did you even look where you were aiming?!"

"I can do it almost instinctively now."

"That is incredible Carinne, I would not want to be on your bad side ever!"

She laughed and they resumed walking to the spot.

"This is good. You can practice here Geoff."

He lowered the cage.

"I've never held one of these. Get ready in case it decides to make a break for it."

Carinne smiled and moved back a bit.

Geoff pulled it out of the cage, and it flapped its wings and struggled a bit but then calmed down.

Geoff looked over at Carinne, turned a bit to give her a better viewing angle then closed his eyes, thought of death and applied pressure to the bird's breast. He put it back in its cage then they waited. Carinne was keeping time when they both noticed the bird starting to swell up, its breast doubled in size in the spot where Geoff applied pressure, then it was as if there was a ball inside of it moving. The bird paced back and forth more actively than before. Its size reduced again then enlarged again pulsating and undulating, then it exploded from the point at which Geoff touched the bird, blood and guts flying out its side and it fell dead.

Geoff had blood and some bird guts on him and was beyond disgusted.

"Ugh, this is fucking disgusting! Do you have anything to clean this mess off me?"

"Yes, and it was about 30 seconds."

Carinne ran to the cabin while Geoff removed his coat. She returned with some towels.

"It works Geoff! You can actually kill things by touching them!!" Carinne was excited.

"Yea, I told you. Crazy, isn't it?"

"It's awesome Geoff, we need to use it immediately!"

"I'm kinda surprised to be honest. I thought you would be taken more aback, but I think I need to practice more. I need more animals, some smaller, some larger. Willhaven wants me to master all skills—which I have been—and this one is no different."

"Your right, we can use the farmers market and maybe catch whatever wildlife is here."

Geoff and Carinne cleaned the mess and made plans for the rest of the weekend, they obtained more chickens, mice and caught a deer. There were other random animals in cages stacked in different parts of the property, all out of view.

Carinne watched Geoff practice the move over and over and she began envisioning Geoff killing Draco. Maybe this was Willhaven's plan all along. All Geoff would need to do is come in close contact with him, apply the move, then leave and no one would know. It's flawless. For the first time in years, she felt hope. She left Geoff to continue his practice while she went to do practice of her own in another part of the yard. She relaxed in the kitchen after several hours of practice. Shortly afterward Geoff completed his practice and made his way over to her.

"I'm really tired, I should get going, it's a long drive back to my place."

"You can stay here Geoff, I don't have another bed, but you can use the sofa. It's a bit old and stiff so it would be ok if you still wanted to leave."

"Let me try it out." Geoff sat on it, moved around then reclined. It was stiff but it would only be for two nights he thought.
"It's fine Carinne, thank you."

They both fell asleep around the same time but about 15 minutes into their sleep a growling woke Carinne, she walked back into the room Geoff was in and the source of the growling. It was the strangest snoring she had ever heard but she did not want to wake him. She pulled the blanket back up to chest as it had slid off a bit and prepared for a long loud night. The next morning Geoff was already awake and practicing. Carinne got up and made breakfast then called him in.

"This smells great, I'm so hungry! Thank you Carinne!"

"The pleasure's all mine Geoff. By the way did you sleep well?"

"I slept like a log, I was so tired I think I just blinked, and it was morning again. How about you?"

"You know you snore. Very loud actually."

"I do?"

"Yes, it only bothered me for a bit but then I ignored it."

"Oh, I had no idea, I don't think I've ever done it before, and I've never been told that I did so maybe it's just all this stress."

"Yea. I'm going to go feed Shadow. I'll be right back."

Geoff was finishing his plate as Carinne stepped out. As he reclined in his seat he heard Carinne scream.

Geoff jumped up and ran towards where Carinne had gone. "What's wrong!" He asked in shock.

"You! You killed Shadow!!"

Geoff looked over at all the dead animals in their cages.

"Shadow?"

Carinne stood in front of one of the cages. It was a different-looking cage. Geoff's face went red, the thought had crossed his mind as to why this cage seemed to be separated from the others, but he ignored that little voice telling him to skip this one.

"Carinne… I… I'm so sorry…"

Carinne took Shadow out of his cage and placed him gently on the floor.

Geoff placed a hand on her shoulder, but she shrugged it off yelling "Don't touch me!"

"I'd better go, I'm very sorry Carinne, I did not…." He stopped speaking, turned and left.

"It's not his fault" she thought, "I was careless and should have told him about Shadow." She had another thought. Darkness was seeping into her consciousness again slowly. But this is only a bird she told herself. It was Shadow, her raven who had saved her life and helped her communicate with the team at VARS. It's more than just a bird. "Pull yourself together…Get over this quick." She chastised herself.

Geoff's car could be heard pulling away and driving off.

***

"Willhaven, are you there?" Geoff called out into the emptiness of the penthouse.
"Geoff, I am here." Willhaven was in a nearby room set up as a second office away from VARS. He walked into the main area to meet Geoff.

"I killed Carinne's raven accidentally with the death touch. It was mixed in with other animals. It was a mistake."

"I see Geoff. I am glad you are practicing but you cannot make mistakes with this ability. You must treat every choice as a life-

or-death choice because it is. As you murder tiny innocent animals consider this because it does not lessen the consequences."

"Murdering?! How else am I supposed to practice!" Geoff became incensed at the words Willhaven chose to describe what he was doing, accurate though they be.

"I am not judging, but it is what it is, and it is an ability I gave you so now you decide who lives and dies and the consequences that come with those decisions."

Geoff was silent. He had not thought of his practicing as murdering, but Willhaven's words were weighing heavily on him. He looked down at his own feet for a moment and considered giving up.

"Geoff, I will teach you another move, possibly even more deadly."

Geoff looked up and blankly stared at Willhaven. "What can be more deadly than death?" He thought.

Willhaven put forward both hands and formed a V shape with them then placed them on Geoff's chest.

"When you do this move you will pull death into yourself. This will negate death for the victim and pass it on to you. You must think that you ARE death when performing it."

Willhaven then reminded Geoff:

"Do not take these abilities lightly, and this won't work on something that is already dead, it must be dying for it to work. I hope this ends any further discussions about these abilities and more importantly no more stupid mistakes Geoff."

"Will, I did not know it was her bird."

"Forget the bird, it taught you a valuable lesson."

Geoff took a step back. Then another and another.

Willhaven smiled and asked rhetorically, what is it Geoff? Do you see something?

"No actually, I don't see something I should be seeing!"

Willhaven crossed his arms.

"That's right Geoff, I have no aura."

"What the fuck is happening!" Geoff thought to himself.

"Geoff, I have a mission for you. Only one. It's a rescue."

Geoff gathered himself again and his composure straightened. "What is my mission?"

"You are to rescue Carinne."

***

Patrick answered his phone, the ring catching him off guard as he was reviewing pictures of new victims the City has spat out at him.

"Hello, this is Detective Warn."

"Hello Detective, I have been assigned to Bobby's appeal. I am one of two lawyers that will be assisting Bobby with his appeal. My name is Morgan Esquival."

"Pleasure to meet you Mr. Esquival. How can I help you."

"We would like to move expeditiously with Bobby's case, if you would be so kind as to provide us a general understanding of the officers involved, historical, personal, anything. I would like to schedule a time to interview you on those details and other details of the case you may have."

"Sure, we can setup a time tomorrow, early afternoon is open for me."

"That's great, thank you for your cooperation. We will speak soon."

"Looks like this case is getting hot again." Patrick thought to himself. He would see where he could help Bobby while being careful regarding information about his so-called peers. As he walked towards the exit, he passed one of the officers involved in obtaining Bobby's testimony, they caught each other's glance, Officer Sezowich threw a professional smile over to Patrick which was returned with a cold stare. As he exited the precinct the thought of helping expedite Bobby's release brought warmth to the otherwise cold day. He looked forward to the interview.

The following day was greeted by gray clouds hiding the sun. This would be the forecast for the next several days with storms highlighting the worst of it. In Patrick's office with the storm as ambiance the discussions would begin. Patrick's interview concluded after several hours, he was surprised at the duration. He never looked at the clock the entire time until it was over. He was fairly certain that he had given enough to cause the right judge to vacate the conviction but then he remembered reality.

"Thank you for your time, Detective. Also, you should be prepared to be called to testify."

"Thank you both as well."

They shook hands and as Bobby's lawyer's left, Patrick grabbed one of his darts and tossed it at his dartboard. The dart landed dead center, bullseye, other darts could be seen impaled on the outer edges. He smiled at his momentary luck and went back to work.

***

Carinne was busy training her gymnastics students. People were in a short line practicing flips. One would step forward, walk onto the mat, get a running start then begin flipping across the mat. One young girl went flipping but lost her balance near the end of her routine, she fell flat on her back then heard Carinne's voice.

"Are you ok Melanie?"

Melanie stood up slowly, she rotated her arms, no pain, she twisted her waist back and forth and also no pain.

"Yep, all good here."

"Ok get back in line, next please."

The next student stepped forward and began his run and flips. He completed them sloppily, the end landing almost causing him to fall.

"Ok Greg, keep at it."

Carinne heard a faint tapping at one of the high windows, a familiar tapping. She looked up and looking back down at her was a large raven.

"It must be Willhaven." She thought. She told her class to take a 10-minute break and stepped outside. She held out her arm and the raven landed. On one of its legs was a note which she gently removed. She petted the raven and gave it treats. Memories of Shadow came flooding back as she released the bird with a raised arm. The note said:

"Dear Carinne, please come see me. We need to talk, urgently."

It was signed ~Will.

Very late that afternoon she flew over to the penthouse with great speed, storm clouds remained making the oncoming night even darker. Willhaven saw her entering the building from his perch up above. As she entered the penthouse area Willhaven turned to greet her.

"Hello Carinne, you are looking mighty pale these days."

"Hello Willhaven, it's good to see you too. And yes, I need to get out more."

"What you need to do is get out of Hope City."

"Will, I can't you know I have unfinished business here."

"I am well aware of your desire to punish Draco. You need to leave that to me. I forbid you to take any action against him directly. For your sake especially Carinne."

"I know what I'm doing Will!"

Willhaven did not change his tone to match her anger. He remained mechanically calm as usual.

"Did you know what you were doing when you got Bobby arrested?"

"Bobby…."

"I will be fixing that shortly so don't worry too much about it, but I am very serious, you need to leave. That brings us to your mission."

"My mission is to punish Draco."

"No Carinne. You need to let go. Draco is too dangerous. He will get what's coming to him. You don't need to worry about him escaping punishment."

"What is my mission Will? What would you like me to do??"

"I need you to save Geoff. Get him out of Hope City. Wherever you both decide to go or do, returning here is not an option. Hell is breaking loose Carinne. There may be a point where you cannot be saved any longer. The same goes for Geoff."

"Will, I want to learn the touch of death."

"Absolutely not. I gave that to Geoff because of how dangerous his task is."

"I don't know if I can leave Will, I just can't."

"I was expecting you to say that. Stay close to Geoff. However, there will come a point when, if you have not left by then, you may join your family."

"WILL! What are you saying."

"I'm saying it's not your time to die, but that may change if you continue to linger. Right now, you must start thinking of tomorrow. A tomorrow far away from Hope City, either with or without Geoff but not here."

"Will, what do you plan to do!"

"I am going to unleash revenge."

"I don't know what you've become Will…"

"Carinne, Willhaven is dead. You are not. Not yet. Please take your mission seriously. Things will be getting very dangerous very soon."

"Goodbye Will."

"I hope so Carinne."

She turned and walked away slowly; her cheeks were wet, small streams flowed downward.

"I don't know what's happened to you Will." She thought to

herself. The emptiness of the penthouse seemed larger than before. The dark day casts more shadows. Willhaven watched her leave. Unfortunately, he was unable to cry or feel emotions on a human level after his alteration. His brain's chemicals were subdued significantly as part of that process, but he still remembered what it should feel like. His stare was fixed on Carinne until she vanished into the hall. He went over to one of the windows and looked down and waited and watched as Carinne walked away slowly. He thought perhaps maybe he was too harsh with her. As he continued to stare at her a car pulls up slowly from behind. Willhaven's adrenaline rises along with his fight response. The artificial intelligence has confirmed that danger is afoot and in the next moment two men jump out from the rear seat of the car and grab Carinne from behind.

"Spirit, can you hear me? What is going on, my senses are all firing at once!"

Willhaven then began to have a vision, it was a row of coffins, in them from left to right were Geoff, Carinne and himself. It was clear that this situation was dire. Willhaven felt more alive now than he has since the operations. The time to fight was now and without wasting another moment he exited the penthouse through the rooftop and began following Carinne's abductors. The car was driving fast but Willhaven had gained and overcame its lead. He was performing massive jumps at great distances and flinging himself using all his arms. While mid-flight he remembered to lower his armored face for combat.

Meanwhile inside the car one of the thugs was speaking to Carinne.

"It's ok sweetie, you hid from us a long time, but I remembered your face."

Carinne spat towards him, but he dodged.

"And to think, all this time, I went lookin for you in other towns, but you were here all along."

"Who are you!" Carinne screamed.

"You don't know me cause we never met officially. I know you though. Man, what a hunt you sent me on. I was looking every which way trying to find you and you were under my damn nose the whole fucking time."

He grabbed her chin and moved her head over to him to force her to stare him in the face, but she jerked away and continued staring forward.

"I get it, I get it, why would you want to look at me. Well let me introduce myself and let's see if that changes your mind. I am the man that killed your brother five or so years ago."

Carinne twisted her stare directly at him now, her eyes were wide and intense. He continued speaking.

"That's better, get a good look at me cause it might be the last face you see."

"NO, cher ami! you will meet your end first!"

"We'll see about that. I wasn't sure it was you at first but then I followed you into your gym and watched a few of your sessions then I remembered. It clicked who you were. Then the name. You didn't even bother to change your name. Well, that mistake is gonna cost you. I have some good news though. If you cooperate, maybe things won't look so bad for you. You know Draco was really pissed at me for not getting him the documents all those years ago. You got me in a lot of hot water. Now we can both make things right again. How does that sound."

Carinne began kicking and fighting in the back seat of the car but the assassin to her right punched her which settled down the commotion. The thug on her left began tying her hands.

The car arrived at its destination, Willhaven was directly above looking down and calculating the situation. Three men emerged from the car and carried Carinne inside the house. Willhaven left the power line alone but cut the phone line. He dropped to ground level and stormed the house. He charged through the front door sending splintering pieces inward. The group carrying Carinne stopped and turned at the sound.

The main assassin released his grip on one of Carinne's arms leaving her to the other two. They caught her before she could fall and tried to wrestle her still as she began fighting again at the opportunity the commotion gave her. The assassin turned to Willhaven's approaching figure with the intent of firing several rounds at him, but he was not fast enough. Willhaven closed the distance, all four of his arms extended. He let out a roar that was identical to a lion's roar just before grabbing the assassin, disarming him and ripping his arms out from the sides. The other thug then released Carinne's arms. Willhaven grabbed her with one set of his arms before she could hit the ground then he grabbed the nearest thug with his other set of arms. He spun around pulling Carinne away from the last thug's grip, her feet pulling the thug in causing him to stumble towards the floor. Willhaven now had his fully armored backside facing the last thug. His coat was armor, and it sat covering his chest which was armored. He is invincible from behind and focused his attention on Carinne. He gently steadied her and ordered her to escape immediately. He released her and as she stepped back, she witnessed Willhaven pummel and hammer the thug locked in his grip into the floor. The first round of pummeling broke his arms and his back, and the second round broke his legs. The floorboards broke from the forces and gunshots could be heard from behind Willhaven. Carinne was not new to violence unfortunately, but what she just witnessed was on a whole other level. She gasped at the sight, held her hand up to her mouth but luckily nothing came out then turned and ran out. Willhaven felt the bullets bouncing off his armor, he then spun around to focus on the last thug. He charged him, grabbed him, then lifted him over his head and slammed him over his knee breaking his back. He then finished him off by snapping his neck. Willhaven cleared the home and ensured no others remained. He then proceeded to dispose of the bodies. They did not have time to contact Draco, so he concluded this situation had been neutralized. A close call to be sure. It is very unfortunate that Carinne had to witness this spectacle but perhaps now she would treat the situation with appropriate regard. Or so Willhaven had hoped. Willhaven needed to focus back on the main mission. He had a busy week ahead of him.

***

The next day lightning was lighting up the sky. Willhaven was on the rooftop across from City Hall. The timing of the weather was also a welcome unexpected boon. It would provide cover and ensure smaller crowds are below. This would be one of very few instances where Willhaven was out during daylight hours. He made sure the doors leading up to the rooftop were double locked. Willhaven had a compound bow and several arrows. Some had bullet tips, and a few had razor sharp broad heads and a couple more had explosive heads. Other shadows had used this same roof top to survey the Mayor's activities and daily routine which they fed back to Willhaven. He had made calculations that allowed him to accurately guess how the mayor would move and where he would be and was now ready with high certainty of the locations the mayor would be in.

"It's time Mr. Lombardi." Willhaven thought to himself, then with his two fully mechanical arms he raised the compound bow, loaded a bullet tipped arrow, aimed, and in another hand, he readied a broad head tipped arrow. Down below Frank walked into his office, sat at his desk and placed a stack of papers on one side of his desk. Thunder cracked outside causing him to look out the window briefly but then he returned to his business of signing documents. He grabbed a pen, pulled over one of the papers, placed the pen down then the crack of breaking glass caught his attention. This was the first arrow Willhaven launched. Frank placed both hands on his desk and a whoosh went past his face; he looked down and an arrow had impaled his signing hand to the desk. Before the pain could register with him another arrow struck the other hand. Frank begins screaming. The arrow penetrated so deeply into the desk that Frank was hopelessly stuck, the extreme pain and bleeding from the broad heads prevented him from even attempting any movement as each slight move sent searing pain up his arm. The sounds of footsteps could be heard which were then interrupted by another crack of thunder then another arrow making impact on the floor, its tip exploding and spreading a noxious gas. The result of which was similar to a pepper gas, Franks eyes were burning, he was coughing in between screams. A police officer tripped and fell as the gas made it hard to see. In the room across the hallway another arrow landed, its tip was on fire, and it began spreading immediately to a stack of paperwork. A reporter Willhaven had ensured received a tip to be at City Hall was outside waiting and a few feet ahead of him a bullet tipped arrow landed with a note attached. Another arrow, this one with an explosive tip flew from Willhaven's bow, through an opening in tree branches, whirred its way to a police cruiser and made contact with the rear portion of the car causing a massive explosion which sent pools of flaming gas everywhere. Everyone, even the reporter looked over. There was mass confusion. Willhaven now having delivered his messages ran to the opposite side of the rooftop, leaped across to another building, the leap was framed by lightning mid jump, but no one saw. He carried the bow in one of his mechanical hands, the rest were free to aid in movement. He disappeared into the distance and was gone before anyone knew he was there. The reporter on the scene having found shelter waited and waited. After some time, he decided the attack was over. He removed the note from the arrow and immediately left the scene as he was instructed. He began reading the note:

"To all Hope City residents, a message was delivered today to your dishonorable Mayor, Frank Lombardi. This is the second

note he has received and has made well to hide the first. Frank has his own note reminding him that his time is running out and now you shall all know as well. Frank is to step down as Mayor and turn himself in to the authorities. He is to confess to crimes too numerous to list all here but to name a few, corruption, assassinations and racketeering."

The note is signed ~Death.

"This is great!" He thought to himself, his big break and this was big news. He headed immediately to the paper where he worked. Meanwhile, Frank was sedated by medics and placed in an ambulance which was escorted to the hospital by two patrol cars. Patrick was already rushing over to the crime scene, the traffic was low due to the bad weather and when he arrived, he saw the two arrows still in Frank's desk but they had been cut to allow Frank to be removed and on them tightly wrapped notes. Photos were taken, officers interviewed, and Patrick took the notes as evidence. When he arrived back at the precinct he opened the notes, they were identical copies. The message was:

"Hello Frank, I took the liberty to make it a much larger spectacle should you try to hide evidence as you did the first time. You will remember, I'm sure, you ignored the first warning you were given at the town hall so here is a reminder. You are to step down as Mayor and surrender to the authorities. You are to confess to your numerous crimes. Your time is running out

Frank. Failure to act on this means the end for you. Do not return to City Hall in any capacity. Doing so will result in your demise."

Patrick took photos of the note, added it to the evidence pile for this crime but also for Bobby's case. He then took a photo to keep as a copy for himself and immediately called Bobby's lawyers.

***

 Frank was lying in a bed in a secure area of the Hope City Hospital. Two officers were guarding the door to his room and only allowed doctors and nurses in. Down in the lobby area there were about half a dozen officers guarding the main entrance by keeping reporters and other undesirables out and maintaining order. The news of Frank's residency caused a group of about twenty or more protesters to form just outside the hospital entrance. The muffled noises from the protesters clashing with the officers below were barely audible to Frank but he was not concerned. He was medicated, drowsy and relaxed. He was also no stranger to protests because as the crime rate soared, so did their numbers. But they could be controlled, divided and subdued. He already knew Draco would provide for counter protesters to discredit anyone getting in his way.

Frank moved his arms over his bed sheet. Pain

seared through them and through the medications. "Did someone open a window?" He thought. Cold air filled the room. Behind Frank a metal finger could be seen slowly raising his window higher and higher until it was raised as far as it would go. Using all four arms and hands Willhaven crawled in like a spider. He crept slowly over to Frank. Frank looked up very drowsily.

"Who are you?"

"I am here to give you more medicine Frank." The voice came low and crackly.

Frank began to tremble. He saw the four arms and a metallic face. All of it was blurry. One of the arms reached out. It was long and the hand's fingers curled into a form that looked like it was pointing at Frank. Then this index finger landed square on his chest and drew a symbol on him. Frank could feel it when it tapped the center of his chest then slid to the right, just under his nipple, then slid down to his belly button then back up to the other side of his chest under his other nipple then back to the center. It was an inverted triangle. Frank was about to yell and the instant his mouth opened wide another metallic hand appeared as if a magician snapped his fingers and it was suddenly there cupping and closing his mouth again.

"No noises Frank. This is only a dream and soon this dream will be over. You have been death marked." The voice cracked.

"One last thing Frank. If you make any sound whatsoever or cause any folly to bring attention here or to us I will throw you out the window. Do you at least understand that?" The voice crackled again.

Willhaven could feel his mouth trying to move.

"Just nod yes Frank…"

Frank nodded accordingly. Another of Willhaven's arms, outside of Frank's line of sight, had been working the drip, it increased the medication. He could see in Frank's eyes it was taking effect then he restored the dosage. Willhaven released Frank's mouth slowly then stepped back. He was silhouetted by the dark of the room and the medications Frank was on.

"Excellent! I wish you a speedy recovery!" Willhaven very lightly tipped his hat and said "Remember Frank, this is only a dream." Then he crawled back out the window and closed it behind him disappearing into the night sky.

***

A few days later Carinne arrived at her gym but there would be no further training.

"Hello Jess, I am resigning today. I'm sorry if this is catching you by surprise but I'm moving."

"Oh! I'm sorry to hear that, but I'm glad you're moving, this city has become very dangerous lately. I think it will be good for you. I wish you the best of luck Carinne."

"Thank you, Jess, please take care of yourself."

They hugged each other tightly then Carinne parted ways waving bye one last time. She jumped in her car and began her long drive out to her cabin to meet up with Geoff. Meanwhile Geoff was still making preparations, everything in his apartment was all in boxes and the movers would be hauling his stuff over to his parents' house a few hours away to be stored for the time being. He took a walk around his apartment thinking about all the years he had been there. He had a strange feeling come over him wondering where he would go next but he would do the apartment hunting with Carinne. They could not stay in Hope City any longer, his mission kept replaying itself in his head. The ringing of the phone stopped his mind from continuing to wander.

"Hello Geoff, this is Willhaven." The voice said as Geoff answered the phone.

"Hello Will I am working on my mission. I have not…"

"Geoff, have you read today's paper?" Willhaven interrupted.

"I have a copy of it but nothing interesting why?"

"Nothing interesting on the front page right?"

Geoff grabbed the paper off the table. As he read it there was a knocking at his door. He turned, answered it and it was the movers.

"Hello, you Geoff?"

"Hi yea, you can start taking all these boxes."

"Sounds good boss."

"Will, there's nothing special on the front page. What is it you want me to see?"

"Go to page 5, bottom left."

"Ok."

He flipped pages quickly, looked in the bottom left and found a small article titled "ATTACK ON CITY HALL."

"WOW, what the hell! Was that you?"

"Indeed, it was, and they hid the story. It should be on page one!"

"Yea…"

"Geoff, this is the level of control they have. You and Carinne need to leave immediately."

"I'm working on it. She has a cabin outside the city limits."

"Geoff, in five days hell will be set loose, if you both are still in the city there are no guarantees that either of you will survive."

"WHAT!"

"Make sure you both are gone and don't ever return am I clear?"

"Will, what the hell is going on?"

"Hell is exactly what's going on. I need to focus on the situation here; I cannot be distracted by either you or Carinne."

"Ok, I don't need to know any more. I am solely focused on my mission."

"You will need the skills I taught you Geoff, be prepared, be strong."

Willhaven hung up after that. Geoff heard a box fall then glass breaking inside.

"Hey, be careful with that!"

"Sorry boss."

Carinne arrived at the cabin with her car packed full of boxes. The cabin was small, but they would only need it temporarily until they found a more permanent home. After the boxes were unloaded and stacked out of the way in the cabin, she decided the targets needed some attention and began practicing her throws. On each target she saw Draco's face. She threw several darts and landed bullseye on all but then paused.

"I have to let go. Geoff and Willhaven are right." She thought to herself as she removed the darts. But again, they landed, and she repeated this a third time. Letting go seems impossible when you have been doing something sunrise to sunset for years. She pulled the darts out, but this time packed them away. Off in the distance Geoff was pulling up. His car was packed with boxes he did not trust the movers with.

They regrouped in the cabin, and both sat at the kitchen table each having some tea. Geoff brought with him good news.

"Hey Carinne, did you hear? Bobby's been released."

"No, I didn't, that's great news."

"Detective Warn added evidence to his case which exonerated him, and his conviction was vacated."

"I'm so glad for Bobby. What was the new evidence?"

"I spoke with Willhaven earlier and he…"

Geoff paused and stirred his tea then took a sip, put the cup down and continued.

"He attacked City Hall, impaled the mayor's hands to his desk using arrows, blew up a squad car and delivered a note to both the mayor and a reporter that was tipped off to be at the scene."

"Oh my GOD! That was so risky of him? He does not usually work during the day."

"He wanted the attention. It was used to put the mayor on alert and the evidence proves that the assassin is still lose so Bobby was set free."

Geoff noticed her hand clutching the teacup, her fingers were turning white from the grip.

"Are you upset Carinne?"

"He should have killed him."

"I think he intends to. It's the reason we need to leave. He said he would let Hell loose in a rather literal manner."

Carinne reached over and grabbed Geoff's hand.

"Your right, I'm trying hard to let go."

"I understand. I am here to help you."

Frank was at his desk at City Hall with both his hands bandaged. He was dictating to a new secretary whose job was to act on his behalf while his hands healed. He had very limited painful movement of his fingers and did his best not to do anything with them. Due to him having to announce everything, he maintained no contact with Draco and behaved totally in opposition to his character. Far off in the distance from a high tower, Willhaven was watching the activities of Frank's arrival through binoculars and he took note of the broken bargain. He expected it, so this was no surprise and now his final actions would be executed. No more warnings. Frank's time had come much like that of many others.

***

"Hello this is the Draco residence how may I help you?"

"This is Mark Pull, I work with Detective Patrick Warn. I would like to speak to Draco."

"One minute sir."

The call was transferred over to Draco who was seated with his feet on his desk.

"Hello this is Draco."

"Hello Draco, Mark Pull here. I have some information for you regarding the attempted murder on Frank."

"Hello Mark, what would this information be?"

"Before I tell you I want to remind you of the deal, ten thousand dollars is what was promised."

"I remember Mark but that is contingent on the value of the information."

"I think this will get you to your assassin(s)." He emphasized the plurality of it to Draco.

"Ok Mark, maybe come here in person and let's discuss. Stop by as soon as you can."

Mark grabbed a bag with the evidence Draco needed then ran out of his house towards his car. As he was walking speedily, he bumped into a very tall figure spilling coffee on his coat. It seemed to Mark however that in the bump the coffee may have been thrown on him, but he could not be sure. The other figure grabbed a handkerchief and started dabbing Mark's chest but only on certain points and traced out some type of outline in the form of a W. The coffee stain's outline showed this.

"What are you doing!" He snapped at the tall figure.

The tall figure didn't speak just waved his hands in front of Mark in a manner suggesting him to calm down and he went back to patting him, trying to clean the coffee. Mark pushed him away but before Mark's hands could land on the tall fellow's chest he immediately stepped back, raised his hands and put the handkerchief away and nodded then walked away. Mark turned back around, frustrated at the delay and changed into a new coat.

Mark arrived at the Amichi Mansion in about an hour, and he was quickly escorted to Draco's office to continue the conversation. They sat across from each other, Draco's face bore an expression of confidence and a small smile. Mark on the other hand was quite stoic, stern and emotionless.

"In this case is your ten thousand Mark. But only if I like what I hear."

"Oh, you will like it."

Draco flipped open the latches and raised the lid enough for Mark to see all the crisp new hundred dollar bills.

"Ok Draco, here it is, Detective Warn whom I'm sure you are familiar with, took evidence from the crime scene and added it to a new case of course, but also to Bobby Gray's case. The evidence was used to free Bobby. If you don't know who that is, he was the lookout during the Town Hall attack. In this bag I have copies of this evidence but more importantly I have added information about Bobby's lawyers. They were paid for by an agency called VARS which stands for Victim Assistance and Relocation Society. I ran a banking check against them, and they have been paying salaries to some people you might be interested in. I can't find job titles and most of their expenditure is in helping victims find new homes and re-establish themselves. The most recent paychecks went out to Carinne Durand and Geoff Bryson. Geoff was a reporter for the local paper."

Draco smiled wildly, placed his hands on the case full of money and slid it over to Mark. Mark in kind placed his bag on the desk and slid it over to Draco.

"It's been a pleasure doing business with you Mark."

"Likewise, Draco."

Draco began making plans to have Bobby brought to him for questioning. Tonight, he would have the identity of the assassins.

Bobby sat down at the dinner table. He received a hug from his mom then she made her way into the kitchen.

"Glad to have you back Bobby. We thought you might be in there a long time." His Dad said.

"I'm glad to be back Dad."

Before his father could take a seat at the table there was a hard knock at the door.

"I wonder who that could be at this time?" His father said as he walked over to the door.

"Who is it?"

"We're here to speak with you and Bobby, it's official business. Let us in."

The door opened slowly but the trespassers pushed their way in once it was unlocked.

3 large men entered with guns drawn.

"NOBODY MAKE ANY LOUD SOUNDS!" one ordered.

Another grabbed the mother and escorted her into another room.

Bobby and his father were forced to sit in their living room. Two more guards stood outside the doorway.

"Listen pops, we're gonna take Bobby here away for a while. We need some questions answered. You and the wife are not gonna call the cops because if you do Bobby here might lose some fingers or maybe a hand. Do we understand each other."

"Y...Y...Yes." Bobby's father stammered.

"Gag him." Ordered the thug.

Bobby's father was tied, gagged and brought into another room.

"Ok, it's your turn Bobby."

They grabbed the boy quickly, tied him up and gagged him. They put a cloth bag over his head and quickly made their way back to the car where Bobby was tossed in the trunk. One thug who stayed behind made his last instruction before leaving.

"Listen wifey, we're gonna leave you and pops here, don't do anything stupid or the boy will pay. If he answers our questions, we'll bring him right back and leave like nothin ever happened. Got me?"

She nodded trembling, then put her head in her hands and started crying and with that they left and the car sped off to a warehouse on the other side of Hope City. When the coast was clear Bobby's mother picked up the phone but instead of calling the police she called the lawyer.

Patrick's and his family just finished their dinner. His son was in his bedroom reading comic books, and his wife was in the kitchen cleaning up after the meal. Patrick was reading case notes when he heard a knock at the door. He went over and moved the cover from the peep hole to see who was there but before he could make out a face the door was kicked in on him and two brute's charged in. They grabbed him, spun him over then began tying him down. A third brute entered but not fast enough before Patrick's wife let out a scream. She was quickly subdued and tied up. His son looked through a crack in the door and saw what was happening to them then jumped out his window and ran to the neighbors. Patrick was carried out with a cloth bag over his head and tossed into the trunk of the car which then drove off immediately. The destination was the Hope City Bridge.

At the entrance to the Bridge rope work that was previously arranged was in place and ready to receive its package. Patrick was pulled out of the trunk, leaned up against the car and his cloth bag removed. He was still gagged and could not speak but his speech was not necessary.
One of the men came up to him. Patrick recognized him as Tony Blanco. The man leaned toward Patrick and with a cold tone said:

"This is for being a good cop, but not good enough."

He grabbed the rope and placed the noose around Patrick's neck. While this was occurring one of the other thugs tied the other end of the rope to the car's bumper. The driver, upon Tony's signal, slowly drove forward lifting Patrick up to the lower rafters of the bridge where he flayed for a few minutes until lifeless. They then tied the other end to the bridge and left him there to be found by his peers.

***

The sunset over the cabin was picturesque despite its solitude. The evening came immediately thereafter bringing with it winds and chills. The cabin's windows had a warm amber glow cast by candlelight from within. Carinne and Geoff had an early dinner and were lost in conversation for a few hours until they both gave in to the sandman's beckoning. Geoff tried sleeping on his side to prevent any snoring from taking place and slept on the sofa again. Carinne was in the back room sound asleep. As the night moved on, she tossed and turned. The cold air of the cabin made sleep easy but also prompted bad dreams for her. The moonlight lit her room just slightly enough to cast frightening shadows in the corners from tree branches swaying in the wind outdoors. In her mind the nightmare has invaded and set the scene.

Carinne is in the Hope City Cemetery, she is standing facing a headstone. The headstone belongs to her brother, Charles Durand. She leans in and places a rose on the ground. A hand bursts from under the earth and grabs her wrist. She tries to free herself by pulling back but it won't let go. Another hand comes out of the darkness behind her and grabs her other wrist. She turns in shock but sees its Geoff tugging her in opposition to the earth-bound hand. As the tug of war continues, Geoff pulls hard enough to force the owner of the earth-bound hand to rise, dirt falling away to reveal a decomposed Charles. Carinne tries to free herself from Charles but loses her balance and falls into an open grave next to her. She falls into an open coffin at the bottom. The last thing she sees is Charles over her as he slams the coffin shut. Carinne tries to push against the lid, but it won't budge. Sounds of rustling against the coffin can be heard. Then it's quiet, then the sounds of gravel crunching can be heard. She wakes, startled, confused. She still hears the sound of gravel crunching outside. A car is pulling up in the dark. She quietly gets dressed faster than she's ever done before and silently creeps quickly to Geoff, gently wakes him, covers his mouth making a "hush" motion with her finger to her lips and he also hears the faint noises outside. They are now both dressed and ready for a fight. Carinne is armed with darts and knives. All sounds stop for a moment. Then, without warning, the front door is thrown open with extreme force. Wood splinters from the door frame fall to the floor, one of the intruders is directly in Geoff's view, Geoff lunges toward him and performs a death touch on him. The thug then begins wrestling Geoff. Immediately behind this thug is another who storms in pushing them aside making his way towards Carinne, she back flips away from him releasing two darts mid flip then lands smoothly, the darts, one in the chest the other in the shoulder of the gun arm causes him to drop his weapon. A third thug stands in the doorway; Geoff manages to free himself from the first thug as death has placed the thug into a state of pain tremors. The thug notices severe pain in his belly and chest, he lifts his shirt to see the skin beginning to rot. Pain now causing him to grab his stomach as he yell's "They got me Kev, kill them all right now! I'm dying!" The third thug, Kevin, is jumped by Geoff who death touches him as well. He pushes Geoff back. He is easily twice Geoff's size. Carinne begins wresting with the injured thug on the floor preventing him from getting the gun he dropped, Geoff landing near to them decides to intervene, Geoff rolls the thug over to expose his chest, and death touches him as well.

"I… I Can't take the pain anymore Kev!! Shoot ME!"

Kevin looks over in shock, the thug's body has swollen, and his face appears necrotic, in the next instant the thug's belly ruptures and his internals spill all over the floor. The injured thug who is now in the throes of this same pain screams out.

"Kevin! HELP ME!!! I'M DYING!!!"

Kevin runs out of the cabin towards the car, the getaway driver wondering what's happening.

"Peter, they did something to me. It hurts; everything hurts!"

He stumbled against the driver's side, arms bent inward hugging his chest. The passenger's side door was opened quietly during the exchange, Carinne was partially in and pointed her sword toward the driver's neck.
"Don't move or I'll cut you open!" She ordered.

Kevin then slumps against the driver's side door and his eyes ooze out of their sockets landing in the car.

"Oh my GOD! What the fuck is happing here!"

"Peter, is it? Listen, you're going to tell us what you're doing here or you will suffer the same fate!" Carinne moved the sword point piercing the skin under Peter's jaw.

Geoff was now in the back seat behind the driver.

"Start talking!" Geoff called.

"Ok ok, we was supposed to grab the girl and bring her to this warehouse. They were gonna interrogate her and the boy to get answers."

"What boy?" Geoff asked

"I dunno, Bobby, I think. They got him tied up for questioning, the girl was next."

"Bobby!" Carinne yelled in shock then she continued:

"Geoff we have to save him!"

"Carinne…. we can't…."

"Geoff! Please!!"

Geoff considered the situation.

"I have a gun pointed to your back, and she has a sword to your neck, do as I say, bring us to this warehouse immediately and silently. You try to get slick, and you will get dead."

The car exited the driveway and sped along the dark roads, Hope City coming into view below the mountain ridge. Geoff looked over at Carinne and started speaking.

"Carinne, I feel funny. Energized in a way."

"I do also."

"No, this is very different Carinne. I can sense more as well."

"What do you mean?"

"Well, our driver here for example. He helped drown a woman who was witness to a murder he was involved in."

"Hey! How did you know that!" The driver called.

"Shut up and keep driving." Carinne gave him a poke with the sword's tip as a reminder.

"I get premonitions, visions now. They are very faded and weak but clear enough that I understand them."

"Are you getting any right now about anything else?" She asked.

"No."

"Drive faster!" she snapped!

***

Over at the Amichi residence Draco is on the phone.

"Call me when you have captured the others. Since it could take a while I'm going to bed early. You will wake me when you have everyone no matter the time." Draco took a sip of red wine finishing off the glass and hung up the phone. He walked over to his bedroom; his wife was already asleep. An open bottle of medicine was by her side of the bed on the table. Draco changed and slipped quietly into bed. Darkness covered the room and Draco was fast asleep.

Tonight, he would get little rest however. His

dreams begin simply, in one of them he was standing over a large supply of drugs in cases ready for their new owners, on a table nearby was a pyramid of money cleanly stacked and in its appropriate wrappers. Before the dream was able to progress anywhere a loud sound caused him to turn face up on his bed, now staring at the ceiling. He looked over at his wife for a moment, but she was still sound asleep. He considered waking her but then another loud sound came. It was the sound of something large and heavy falling. "Someone's broken in!" he thought to himself. He leaned over to wake his wife and as he nudged her quietly and whispered to her, he received no response. He tried again and she let out a snore growl that caused Draco to pull back a moment. He leaned in again and slowly removed the blanket, as it moved away the figure underneath was shown to be a corpse, it turned to face Draco, and he fell out of bed and quickly crawled on his knees to the door. He turned back around to catch a glimpse of the corpse beginning to rise, growing as it does so, it sat and faced him again. Draco stood up and went out into the hallway, closed the door behind him and went to his office and grabbed his gun. The noise of something else breaking came from downstairs again. He ran out and looked down at his curved staircase. He could see one of his statues had fallen off or was knocked off. Where a cherub had been was now empty. He did not notice any pieces on the floor. "Probably someone stealing it?" he thought, but it was very heavy marble and somewhat large. He begins descending the staircase slowly and begins hearing a harp. The notes ring from high to low then repeat three more times and a song begins playing. Draco recognizes the song as Danse Macabre by Camille Saint-Saëns. He moves to the 1st floor and looking down at the open area in the living room he begins to see a harp. The harp has a head carved on the front in Roman style. He moves slowly some more and reveals more of the harp, and he can now see hands plucking away. The arms are fat, and the fingers are like a child's but an overgrown child. He moves more to the side and now as he begins to see more it starts speaking to him in a child's voice.

"Draco, the dance has begun."

Draco stops movement, points his gun and as he slides more the side profile of the harp is now fully in view but the figure playing the harp gives Draco its backside. It looks like a living Cherub, but the wings are black, they are shadows in the form of wings, slightly translucent. The thing drops from its stool knocking over the harp which falls with a loud thud. The thing then runs back into the darkness and speaks again.

"Draco, are you ready to dance yet? It has begun! Would you like a drink to take the edge off?" It says in a child's voice again.

A light comes on in the next room opposite where the creature went. Draco makes his way into the room slowly; the light is shining dimly over a table. On the table is a single gold goblet adorned with 4 large rubies on its sides. Draco walks up to it and sees red wine in the glass. He cannot resist himself and raises it to his nose. It is the most divine smelling red wine he has ever experienced. All fear drops for a moment as he takes a big sip. Before he could swallow it he immediately noticed the taste did not match the smell at all. It tasted like rot, like puss. The smell now changed as well matching the taste. He spit it out immediately and began gagging. Looking into the goblet again the liquid is thick and black like oil. He drops it and the voice comes again.

"Draaaaco, are you ready to dance now? It's time."

"Who the fuck are you! Show yourself." He yelled, pointing the gun at where the voice came from. He began following the source of the sound and saw the Cherubic creature again but only for a moment, its face still a blur, it runs off into another room. Draco follows it, he can see it now somewhat clearly but still obscured by the darkness. Draco goes to turn on the light, it comes on for a brief moment before the bulb pops and breaks. In that moment Draco caught a good view of the creature, it's face is disfigured but childlike. It was large but in a baby's body, pale white. It wore a black sash around its waist draped down to just above its knees. Where he previously saw shadows for wings were now fully formed wings with black feathers that have a radiant dark blue and very faint dark green to them and they were undulating up and down. The creatures' facial features were more terrifying, it wore a long wide smile filled with two or more rows of needle-sharp teeth, black hollowed out eye sockets with a dim red glow emanating from a central dot and no eyebrows. Draco fired his gun out of terror when the visage registered with his brain, but the gunshot was in darkness, and he could not be sure it was a direct hit. Draco heard the wings flapping quickly so it was still alive. Having lost sight of it he turns to leave the room and hanging from the doorway with one hand the creature, now face to face with Draco bites him quickly on the lips. The nightmare ends, for now, and Draco wakes and falls out of bed sweating.

***

The moon cast a somber glow over the city. Ravens could be seen gathering on all the electrical wires and lamp posts. Outside the 45th Precinct an officer ending his shift lights a cigarette and looks up to see hundreds upon hundreds of ravens perched above him.

"Man, that's weird" he said under his breath.

In the center of the city a giant swarm of birds could be heard rustling and flapping in the night by eventgoers leaving a play that just concluded. They were huddled on the sidewalk exiting the theater and could see the birds, they numbered in the thousands and were perched anywhere and everywhere high up above. More flocks could be seen in the distance silhouetted against the moon. The penthouse area was full of ravens both outside covering the roof top and hundreds within the upper areas of the penthouse. The windows had been left open by Willhaven to let them in.

In the factory district, ravens were amassed in staggering numbers and were nearly invisible in the darkened streets. This district was deserted after working hours and only one building had any activity tonight. In that building is where Bobby was being held and on its roof top its occupants could hear significant rustling and flapping of the birds arrival. Within the facility they were waiting patiently for their drivers to return. The phone rings and one of their leaders' answers.

"Hello?"

"This is Draco, do we have everyone yet?"

"Nah, just the boy. The others are still out. I thought you were sleepin?"

"I am going to be heading down. I can't sleep."

They disconnected. Two more cars pulled up filled with armed gangsters. They made their way quietly into the warehouse and took guard positions at all the entrances. The only witness to this activity being the ravens above.

"Bale, is that you up in the rafters?" Willhaven was looking up hearing the sounds of the ravens rustling. It appeared to be caused by someone moving them out of his or her way.

"Yes, I am here. I ignored your warnings. I think you knew I would."

"Bale, you have chosen death by doing so…"

"I know, I am ready, I am willing, and we will fight together to the end."

"Are you alone?"

"No, Grave is here also."

"Hello Will." Grave's voice was low and metallic compared to Bale's deeper voice.

"I see two cars have pulled up. I can see people leaving them Will." Grave said.

"It seems we have been discovered or been given away." Willhaven replied crackly and stoic.

"A third car just pulled up!" Grave spotted it from his perch up above in the darkness.

"They will be heavily armed, prepare for battle." Willhaven said.

Willhaven walked off and disappeared into the darkness. Bale and Grave began lowering all the blinds to darken the penthouse further. Off in the hallway an elevator door is heard opening, then a second elevator door then many footsteps shuffling.

The penthouse was silent, Willhaven's hearing was better than any humans' due to his Artificial Intelligence having its own microphone acting as another more acute set of ears.

"Get your guns ready, I'm gonna flip the lights." One voice said.

Click, Click, Click.

"Damn, it's not working."

A more brazen thug in the group carefully stepped into the darkened area.

"I'm gonna lift these blinds." He said as he creeped towards them.

He starts raising one set of blinds, at about halfway up Bale jumps down on him sending his sword straight into the thugs back and the tip emerging through the chest. He begins to pull the sword out as the thug begins screaming. One of the other thugs sees Bale's shadowy figure and opens fire from his machine gun. Bale back flips into the darkness, the gun has shattered some of the windows and destroyed the blinds.

"What the fuck!" Another voice yelled and he starts shooting into a random corner of the room. Something jumps in the darkness high up.

The group now looks up and begins firing into the rafters, sending dozens of dead birds falling around them. The new group of thugs that exited the elevator crouched down hearing the gunshots in the penthouse area and drew their guns. Behind them an elevator door opens and one of the thugs looks back and says:

"Hey, who else is coming?"

"Nobody, were all here." Another voice responded then also turns back, both get hit with large darts landing between the eyes. They both fall to the ground. More darts fly out from a figure standing between the elevator and the hallway area who then retreats back into the elevator as the rest of the group of thugs turns around and begins heading back to the elevator area. Grave pushes the button to send the elevator back up to the penthouse and climbs up through the ceiling into the elevator roof riding it up. He prepares a grenade, arms it then waits. The doors open, two guns point inward as the thugs check the elevator. Grave throws the armed grenade from his perch atop the elevator so that it bounces into the hallway and the two thugs follow the noise, see that it's a grenade and dive into the elevator for cover.

"GRENADE!" One of them yelled as the elevator doors closed.

Grave then armed a second grenade, cooked it for 1 second and dropped in with them and immediately made his way up towards the penthouse again. Shouts could be heard in the elevator cabin then the explosion.

Back in the penthouse area Willhaven dropped from the rafters behind one of the thugs firing randomly in front of himself into the darkness.

The muzzle flashes lighting the area only enough to see hundreds of birds above and nothing else. One of Willhaven's hands wrapped around over the thug's mouth and one of his arms placed him into a bear hug. The other two arms took the machine gun in hand and as Willhaven walked backwards putting him further behind the group he began firing into the thug cluster. Several of them fell dead, the others fled into the hallway clumsily encountering the other group which then fired knee-jerk into them killing a few more. Bale climbed out one of the windows and scaled his way over to the window looking into the hallway. He did not notice an armed thug below looking up, the sounds of gunfire having caught his attention.

"Hey, look up there, you see that!" One of them said standing watch over the car.

"Yea, shoot him!" Said the other.

They pulled out their machine guns and began firing. Bale was hit twice in his chest, lost his grip and began to fall.

"Hey, watch out he's gonna hit us!" One of the thugs yelled.

They both ran off to the sides to avoid catching Bales falling body which landed on one of their cars.

"Fuck man!"

"You think we should go up?" Said the other.

"No, we wait here like we were instructed."

Back in the hallway above the thugs reclaim their composure enough to make a plan. They split up into three groups. One group covers the far side of the elevator hallway and the other covers the rear and the last stays covering the penthouse doorway.

The elevator door begins to open, one of the thugs dove in expecting more grenades to be lobbed into the hallway area, he lands on his back clumsily but also fortuitously. He sees the ceiling is opened and he sees Grave's visage just barely and begins firing. Having already landed in an opportune position with the gun already pointing upwards he only needed to pull the trigger and pull the trigger he did. Grave jumped back at the sight trying to dodge but he was not fast enough. One bullet from the spray hit his shoulder causing him to scream and another went into the head causing him to fall through the opening.

Willhaven heard Grave's final scream. He began walking towards the shattered window which was closest to the entrance. He looked out the window and down below he could see Bales' body getting pulled off of one of the cars. He was alone now. He could work undisturbed. He snapped the neck of the thug he had in his grip. He kept his glance at the doorway. Waited a moment. A thug's head popped out to scan the penthouse area and with instant reaction he was impaled with one of Willhaven's darts. It went in one eye causing him to fall back and scream loud enough that they thought the cops might hear on the other end of the city. Willhaven used this distraction to aim and toss the body out the window. The fabric of the dead thug's coat was flapping as the lifeless corpse fell. One of the thugs below heard the flapping sound and looked up just in time to get crushed.

"Holy Fuck and Shit!" The other called out looking up but he saw nothing there to fire at.

Back up at the penthouse Willhaven began walking towards the entrance. He removed the cloak covering his upper body for ease of quick movement. His lower mechanical arms assumed a firing position. The forearms expanded revealing a gun muzzle on each arm and rows of bullets within the forearm. Everyone was a target for death now. His other arms he used to pull down a metal mask concealed within his hat. This would offer significant protection from lucky shots. He had little concern about it as his mechanical brain still made computations for optimum success. As he approached the doorway the thugs could hear his heavy mathematical steps approaching.

"Is he fucking coming out here?" one whispered.

Willhaven tossed a smoke grenade into the hallway and as he approached the threshold, he tossed a second one off the wall sending it way back down the hallway. His AI had locked their positions based on their breathing; any sounds they made speaking and their footsteps. Willhaven was completely covered in smoke and the computation engine estimated that 15 were still alive or somewhat alive and recommended a spray of fire drawing a line of death it had computed based on their detected positions. All these decisions were made in an instant, less than the blink of an eye.

Willhaven used the mini-gun's in his arms and sprayed the hall clear of thugs. Some managed to get out of the way by attempting to retreat at the sounds but they were instantly detected and killed. Willhaven paused for a second to try to sense any life, but both his own senses and his bionics confirmed success. He made his way down the staircase by dropping several floors at a time reaching the lobby area in 4 seconds. As he approached the doorway he could see the one driver left dragging the body of his comrade onto the sidewalk. He was surprised at the fact that this fool remained, but it would save Willhaven a lot of time. As he stepped out into the cold his footsteps were heard as each foot mechanically impacted the stone steps of the entryway. The thug looked over and before he could pull his gun out; one of Willhaven's hands had launched a dart at him at high speed. It knocked the gun out of his hand and with a jump forward, Willhaven closed the distance and grabbed the thug.

"You will tell me everything you know and waste not one breath on me with lies. I have killed over a dozen of your men and unfortunately lost two of my best, but I will not be deterred."

"I don't know anything man I'm just the driver."

Willhaven then lifted him with his two top arms well above his head and his two lower arms reached down and removed one of his shoes and sock. He grabbed the thug's big toe in between his mechanical thumb and index finger. The cold of the metal signifying to the thug that Willhaven meant business.

"I am going to grind your toes into pulp and force you to eat it."

Willhaven began applying pressure and kept applying pressure very slowly. The thug began screaming.

"Stop Stop Stop, I'll talk I'll talk."

The pressure now broke the bone.

"Ahhhhoooowwww! Ok Ok Ok! We got the Kid, He's in a warehouse, we got the girl too and we killed the detective and it's all….OOOWWW STOP STOP STOP."

Willhaven stopped, the big toe now terribly deformed but salvageable.
"Go on." Willhaven said.

The driver laid it all out, everything he knew.
"Is that all?" He asked in a very low tone which was over emphasized by his voice box.

"Yes, that's everything. Please let me go."

"We are not done yet. You will take me as fast as you can to this warehouse. Then I will release you."

They got in the car and drove off, tires screeching. Bobby lay on a table bound and gagged. Just outside of the warehouse Draco steps out of the rear door of a car followed by two others, one from the passenger side and another also from the back door then the driver exited but stood watch over the car. Draco made his way over to Bobby in the back area of the warehouse.

"So, you must be Bobby."

Grumbling could be heard through the gag around Bobby's mouth.

"Well, listen Bobby, everything is going to be ok, and no one will get hurt if you cooperate."

Bobby had heard this before, and he would not be fooled again. Another car stops about a block from the warehouse. Carinne lightly stabs the driver with a dart, its tip coated with a strong sedative.

"Hey, what was that for?"

"It's for your safety." She said as she put the sword away.

The driver began nodding off and both Carinne and Geoff leave the car then begin climbing to the rooftops.

"Over there!" Geoff called.

"Yea, I see it, the only one with lights on."

They made their way slowly over to the warehouse and as they got closer, they heard another car pulling up alongside the one they just left.

"I think we've been found out." Geoff said looking down.

In the other car the driver looks over into the car Carinne and Geoff just vacated.

"That's Danny! Somethings up!" The other driver said.

"Interesting." Came Willhaven's reply.

Willhaven stepped out of the car momentarily, taking a big but calculated risk.

"It's.... It's Willhaven!" She said grabbing Geoff.

"Figures he would be here."

Carinne pulled out a dart and tied a green cloth to it then tossed it into the hood of the car. Down below, the impact noise got both the driver and Willhaven's attention. Willhaven pulled the dart out, closed his hand around it and under his breath said "Carinne…" with sadness. He turned back towards the driver who retrieved a spare gun from under his seat. A shot was fired at point blank range, the bullet deflected off of Willhaven's armored coat, it caused no physical damage but removed the surprise entrance Willhaven had hoped to make. The driver fired all the rounds, emptying the gun then throwing the gun at Willhaven which was dodged. The driver turned to run but with the damaged foot only managed to limp away. Willhaven closed distance instantly, grabbed him, spun him around then using his pointer finger once more traced the mark of death on him then released him.

"You will go and find a nice place to die. You have a couple of hours at most."

Then Willhaven turned and began climbing to the rooftops to meet Carinne and Geoff. He was up to them in no less than 5 seconds.

"I am very disappointed to see you both here despite my warnings."

Geoff was silent.

"Will, we have to save Bobby."

"He may be beyond saving but that is for me to determine. Your being here can only jeopardize this."

"I'm sorry Will but I couldn't…"

"I know Carinne, we are all going through a lot of pain. Stay up high and away from that warehouse. I will attempt to save Bobby. It is important that you both leave, or you will not survive what is coming. I forbid both of you to get any further involved in this, but it will be your choices from now on."

"We understand Will. We will stay up high and try to support you." Geoff grabbed Carinne's hand as he said this, looked over to her briefly and she nodded back.

"Why did you let the driver go?" Geoff questioned.

"I did not let him go. I have marked him for death as I have been doing all along."

Several ravens began landing around them. Three tried landing on Willhaven but he guided them off onto the roof top and several tried landing on Geoff and Carinne as well.

"You see all these birds; I have summoned them here. They will deliver the final blow for me."

"What do you mean!" Exclaimed Carinne.

"You both will see very soon…Unfortunately. When the time comes, you must, at the fastest you have ever moved, escape this city or you will both die."

He turned and began making his way towards the warehouse. They both turned and followed him as well but as promised, stayed high up.

Birds were landing everywhere. Flocks could now be seen far off in the distance landing elsewhere. Willhaven broke off and went right and signaled to them to go left. He dropped down to the lower roof tops then dropped down again and he was on top of the warehouse. Dozens of guards could be seen guarding the entrance and it would be accurate to assume, Willhaven thought, that dozens more would be within. The driver now could be seen running up to the entrance and alerting the guards. More lights were being turned on in and around the building. The element of surprise is gone. Oh well, through the front door it is but first let's cut the power. Willhaven made his way to the main electrical lines and with one chop from his powerful arm severed the line. A loud snap and sparks went flying everywhere. He quickly jumped and ran to the backup line and made a motion with his arms causing the flock of ravens that had perched there to relocate. The sounds of the birds alerted several of the guards below causing them to look up. They spot Willhaven just long enough to train their guns on him as he snaps the electrical line. They fire and his armor deflects the bullets from the machine guns. He pulls back out of view, then drops down into the adjacent alley which was very tight. He had just enough room to squeeze past the row of dumpsters making his way up to the guards that still had their machine guns trained on the rooftop where he was just seconds ago. He jumps onto the platform, putting him on the same level and now they start aiming for him. He manages to cave in the skull of the thug nearest him and holds his lifeless body as an additional shield as he jumps to his next target. He forcefully disarms him as he fires recklessly into the corpse of his buddy. Willhaven slams him to the ground with his free arms and crushes his head like a watermelon using his foot. The force of the blow causing flesh and brain to splatter out sideways. He then begins firing the gun he just acquired, mowing down the other thugs that were in his view. The noise from this skirmish caused another group to make their way towards Willhaven but he drops the corpse shield and climbs up to the second-floor windows of the warehouse loading dock before the other group of thugs can spot him. As they look at the bodies of the fallen, Willhaven has armed and cooked a grenade. He looks down and tosses it, taking advantage of the fact that they remained clumped together as they arrived on the scene. The blast kills all but two which Willhaven finishes off with two gunshots to the head of each. He breaks the window and is now in the warehouse.

Back in the rear of the warehouse Geoff and Carinne have taken advantage of the commotion to break into one of the upper floors. They can see straight down into an open area and tables, some are empty, and one has Bobby on it. Draco is pacing back and forth.

Carinne knew that one of those tables was reserved for her. She began to move but Geoff grabbed her arm and pulled her back. The warehouse was very dark, but their eyes were used to it and worked well. Down below Draco could be seen waving some guards over to the front of the warehouse where the commotion was. They were holding rocket-propelled grenades.

"Oh no! They will Kill him!" Geoff whispered. "I have to do something."

Now it was Carinne pulling him back.

Off in the darkness Willhaven was quickly making his way to the center of the warehouse. One of the guards sees something moving in the darkness and decides to fire his rpg. Willhaven spots him and begins a dodge, but the blast knocks him off causing him to fall into the open area of the warehouse. He manages to stand to the sound of machine gun fire. His coat blocks the attack, and he uses the opportunity to jump back up to a higher spot. On his way up he free's another grenade which he drops on a group of 3 machine gunners. He runs back to put distance between him and the rpg gunner then using the darkness to obscure himself he locates the other rpg gunner and tosses a dart into his head killing him instantly. He sprints over and claims the rpg for himself and begins scanning the area, identifies the other rpg gunner and launches one of the rockets towards him. The explosion kills the other gunner and a few other machine gunners that were nearby. Draco standing over Bobby removes the gag then cuts off one of Bobby's fingers, the pinky.

"Bobby's screams stop the scuffle as everyone looks over to the table in the distance."

"Can you hear me assassin! Surrender now. I am going to kill Bobby slowly if you don't give yourself up!"

It was hard for Draco to yell over Bobby's screams, but Willhaven heard.

Out of the darkness an empty rpg gun is tossed towards Draco which he stops with his foot as it slid across the floor.

"Everybody put your guns down, let him surrender."

Willhaven's footsteps could be heard as he slowly emerges from darkness into the moonlight's rays shining down from the windows. He steps slowly over to Draco with two hands up. The other two arms concealed under his coat. He stops walking about 20 feet away.

"Let him go now or I won't take a step further." Willhaven calls out.

Draco lets out a short laugh.

"Cut him loose, we have whom we want."

Willhaven looks at Bobby then points to a staircase leading up to the rooftop. Willhaven resumes his walk as Bobby runs up the stairs in the darkness. As he approaches the table Bobby was tied to he stops, picks up Bobby's pinky finger then lets out a whistle. A raven emerges and he hands the finger to the raven which then disappears back into the warehouse heights.

"Nice trick's you have." Draco said with a sinister smile on his face.

He had a great feeling of satisfaction now having won against probably an opponent that had been disrupting his business for GOD knows how long.

Willhaven was now standing directly in front of Draco. Willhaven was 6'7" total height. Draco, though not short himself, still had to look up. Before Draco could utter another word Willhaven's second set of arms came out from under his coat. Everything that happens next appeared to all spectators like slow motion. The presence of Willhaven's second set of arms, having caught Draco and the others entirely by surprise, reach out and grab him, one arm on the throat the other on the hand holding the gun. With a snap, Willhaven flicks the gun out of Draco's hand using his mechanical thumb. It was effortless. Then he leans in closer to Draco.

"My name is Willhaven, you may not remember your victims, but you should remember me. You destroyed my arms and legs and left me to bleed to death. Unfortunately for you, the part of me that gave a fuck died and all that was left was revenge."

Draco's eyes widened at the revelation. Willhaven still with two of his arms raised had kept the illusion of surrender in play but this would end now. The third arm lowered and wrestled Draco's other arm to his side, then Willhaven put his foot into Draco's chest, lowered him to the ground while keeping pressure on his chest and Draco's arm's pinned, he readjusted all arms so that his lower arms maintained the pin on Draco and his top two arms began to tear Draco's head off, slowly, deliberately, painfully. Willhaven's fingers dug into Draco's neck. The screams were the loudest any of these seasoned thugs had ever heard. All stared in shock and awe as Draco's head was slowly removed from his body. The visage of Draco's gaping mouth and up swept eyes sent enough terror into the group immediately present to drop their arms and run. Willhaven raises Draco's head up high for Carinne and Geoff to see. Then he unleashes a loud prolonged whistle that enrages all the ravens within ear shot. It was a whistle that went from a low tone to a mid then a high and the high had a vibrato to it that lasted a few seconds. The ravens on the rooftop all flew up, very high up, and formed a funnel of black that looked like a tornado as they descended back down. This was a visual queue for the flocks that were not within range to hear Willhaven's death whistle. When other ravens within view picked up on the strange flock formation, they became ravenous as well, formed their own funnel up high then swooped down targeting first anyone that had been death marked then anyone that just happened to be. This had a chain effect all around the city.

Carinne wanted to collect Draco's head, but Geoff was tugging at her to leave.

"We have to leave Carinne! Let's go."

They had Bobby's finger and left with him heading back to the car quickly. As they climbed out onto the roof, a thug—not present for the other festivities and unaware of what had just happened—fired a shot that luck carried to its mark. Carinne was hit in the stomach. She let out a scream which Willhaven heard causing him to look up and begin to make his way to find her. Geoff, seeing the gunman and hearing the scream immediately threw caution to the wind and dove for him. He performed a death touch quicker than ever before, disarmed the gunman then ran back to Carinne while the thug entered his death throes.

"Carinne...Where were you hit!!"

She pointed to her waist. Geoff began removing her wraps to expose the armor below. He opened her armored vest. The bullet hit in the one area that was not protected in between the folds of the armor. The luckiest shot ever.

"No NO NO!" Geoff yelled in a panic.

He grabbed one of Carinne's hands squeezing it tightly and she also squeezed hard.

He tried to stop the bleeding, but the wound was deep.

"Geoff, it hurts so bad. It's so cold!"

"Carinne, don't die!"

Geoff could feel her grip weakening. He knew she would not make it.

He was thinking panicking. Looking around. Then it came to him.

Carinne was looking at Geoff and noticed a change in his demeanor. A calmness came over him. He let go of her hand, closed his eyes and formed a V shape with his hands and performed the death reversal Willhaven had taught him, then pulled death into himself. He was not sure it would work but there was nothing else left to try. Through her blurry vision she saw Geoff collapse on to the rooftop and begin to convulse. Her vision began to clear. Her pain subsided. It was now Geoff that was dying. Her wound had spit out the bullet and closed. She leaned over Geoff and saw his skin beginning to rot and his chest was heaving up and down as he convulsed. Willhaven had arrived and he walked over to Carinne and looked at Geoff. He knew what had happened.

"Carinne, you won't understand what's going to happen, but I need you to trust me. I need you to do exactly what I say."

"I will do anything, please just save him if you can!"

Willhaven steadied Geoff then performing the same move he taught him and pulled death into himself.

"Willhaven!" Carinne screamed.

"Carinne…" Geoff responded at the scream.

Geoff rose up as he recovered.

"WIllhaven why!?"

"We…We are not done yet Geoff. I need one last favor from you."

"Willhaven your dying!"

"I need you to perform the death touch on me NOW!"

"WHAT!?"

"Geoff, I am already dying, you will understand why later but do it and do it now!"

Geoff nodded.

"Willhaven, I don't see an aura for you, how do I do it."

"Just think it and touch the center of my chest."

Geoff did as he was instructed. He turned to Carinne and said:

"Get to the car with Bobby if we are to save his finger. I will meet you back at the cabin!"

Carinne grabbed Bobby and headed for the hospital.

Geoff watched as Willhaven began shutting down.

"Thank you Geoff. My mission is a success. Leave the city immediately. The birds will try to attack you after they have run out of marked targets, guard your face first and foremost." The voice box was failing, and blood began oozing out of Willhaven's nose and mouth. As he lay dying, he removed his coat and lay on his stomach. He made another death whistle and so began another raven attack, this time on Willhaven. A giant raven swooped down, a bird so large that Geoff had mistaken it for a vulture. It had glowing blue eyes. It landed a few feet away then hopped over to Willhaven. It pecked and pecked and pecked at the back of Willhaven's neck until finally it stopped, angled it's head back and forth and with some sparks jumping from Willhaven's neck pulled the chip out of Willhaven and flew off. Willhaven lay lifeless as the flock attacked.

Off in the distance 4 shadows appeared. One signaled to Geoff to leave, then they claimed Willhaven's remains brushing off the ravens. It took all four to carry him off.

Geoff now began having a vision. He could see the events that were happening in the city. At the far end at Mark Pull's home Mark wakes to the sound of breaking glass. He gets up from bed and walks over to the front door entryway and there is a raven, injured, lying on the floor, wings flapping helplessly. Then about 6 more fly through the broken window and begin attacking Mark, his screams awaken his wife. She runs over to him and with a broom tries to knock the birds off but more fly through the window and now begin attacking her as well. They peck and pull at the skin around the neck and face relentlessly. Over on the other side of town a funnel of birds makes its way down the chimney stack and into the main room of Stephen Kline's home. Waking to the sound of birds flapping in one of his rooms he jumps out of bed and as he enters the hallway he is assaulted by a dozen of them covering his entire body. He opens his mouth to scream but as he was not protecting his face well enough, two birds attack there and fight for his tongue. They pull it to pieces as he gurgles and gets eaten alive.

The last vision Geoff sees is tapping at someone's front door. Frank Lombardi walks up to the door and hears dozens and dozens of taps.

"Who the fuck is this so late at night!" Frank thought.

"Who's there!" He yells. He hears a muffled scream from one of the officers that was guarding the entryway. He starts walking back slowly and an officer breaks the front door open, he is covered in birds, and his partner is lying on the ground also covered in birds. Dozens of the flock enter behind him and begin attacking Frank. They peck at his bandaged hands, peeling away the bandages quickly then the skin then the wound opening it back up again. They begin pecking at his eyelids, pulling away the soft skin then eating his eyes out. The entire time Frank is unable to scream because one of the birds stuck its head far into Franks mouth pecking away at his inner throat.

Geoff stumbled back at the visions then once he got his composure made haste for one of the cars. He scaled quickly down the side of the building but on his way down he began getting attacked as well. He jumped from where he was which was not too far up, maybe 15 feet, dropped and rolled. He made his way to one of the cars, but it was locked. Bodies of guards lay everywhere all were getting feasted on by the ravens. He covered his face, and his armor protected the rest of his body. He made his way to a second car then sped off towards the cabin. Meanwhile Carinne had just left Bobby at the hospital. The bird swarms were everywhere attacking everything that was moving.

"Miss, we think you should stay here in the hospital to be safe." One of the orderlies said to her.

"I can't, I have another emergency I need to take care of." And she ran out the front door. She passed people running in with lots of injuries. Some were lying on the sidewalk nearly having made it to the hospital's front gates. She began getting attacked and protected her face. The car was not far. She jumped in and began speeding towards the cabin.

Geoff was on edge peeking through the windows as Carinne pulled up. When he recognized her, he ran out and she jumped out the car gave him a hug.

"Are you ok?" Geoff asked.

"I'm ok Geoff, what about you?"

"Also ok. What about Bobby?"

"He's at the hospital getting treated, they think they will be able to re-attach his finger."

"That's good news."

As he was holding Carinne's arms another vision came to him. It was Carinne's brother.

"Geoff, I can't thank you enough! You saved my sister. I wish I could be there to thank you in person! Tell her I love her." Then Charles faded away.

"Carinne?"

"What is it Geoff?"

"I just had another vision, several earlier also but this one was your brother."